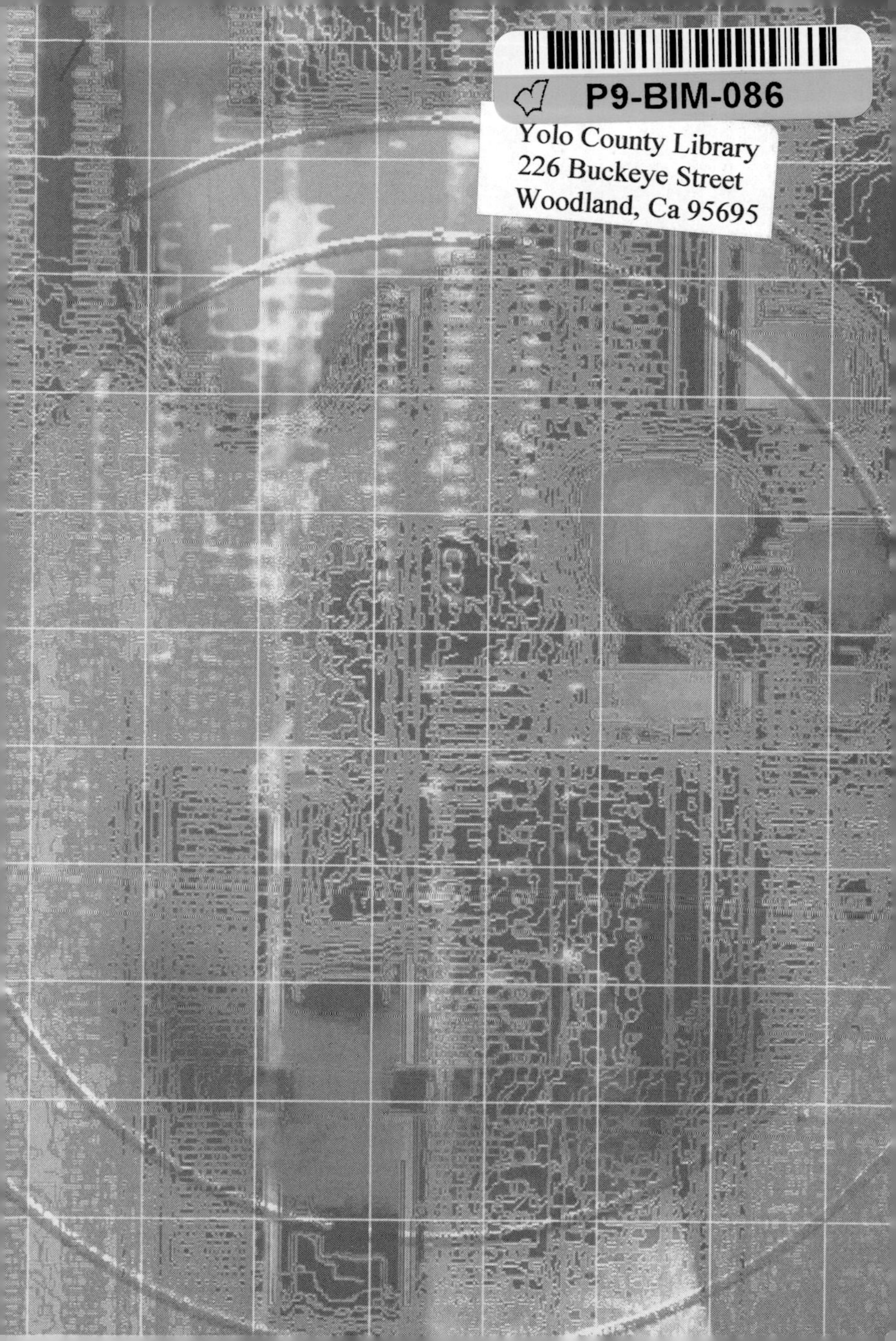

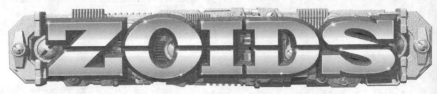

ZOIDS
Chaotic Century
Volume 12

Story and Art by **MICHIRO UEYAMA**

English Adaptation & Editing: William Flanagan
Translator: Kaori Kawakubo Inoue
Touch-up & Lettering: Dan Nakrosis
Cover Design/Benjamin Wright
Graphics & Design/Hidemi Sahara

Managing Editor: Annette Roman
VP of Sales & Marketing: Rick Bauer
VP of Editorial: Hyoe Narita
Publisher: Seiji Horibuchi

Printed in Canada.

Published by VIZ, LLC.
P.O. Box 77010 • San Francisco, CA 94107

10 9 8 7 6 5 4 3 2 1
First printing, January 2003

WHY IS IT BACKWARDS?

ZOIDS was originally a Japanese comic (manga), and since the Japanese read right-to-left, the comic you're reading is a mirror image of the original drawings. So if you noticed that the mark on Van's face is on the wrong side, that's why.

ZOIDS

Chaotic Century
Volume 12

Story and Art by
MICHIRO UEYAMA

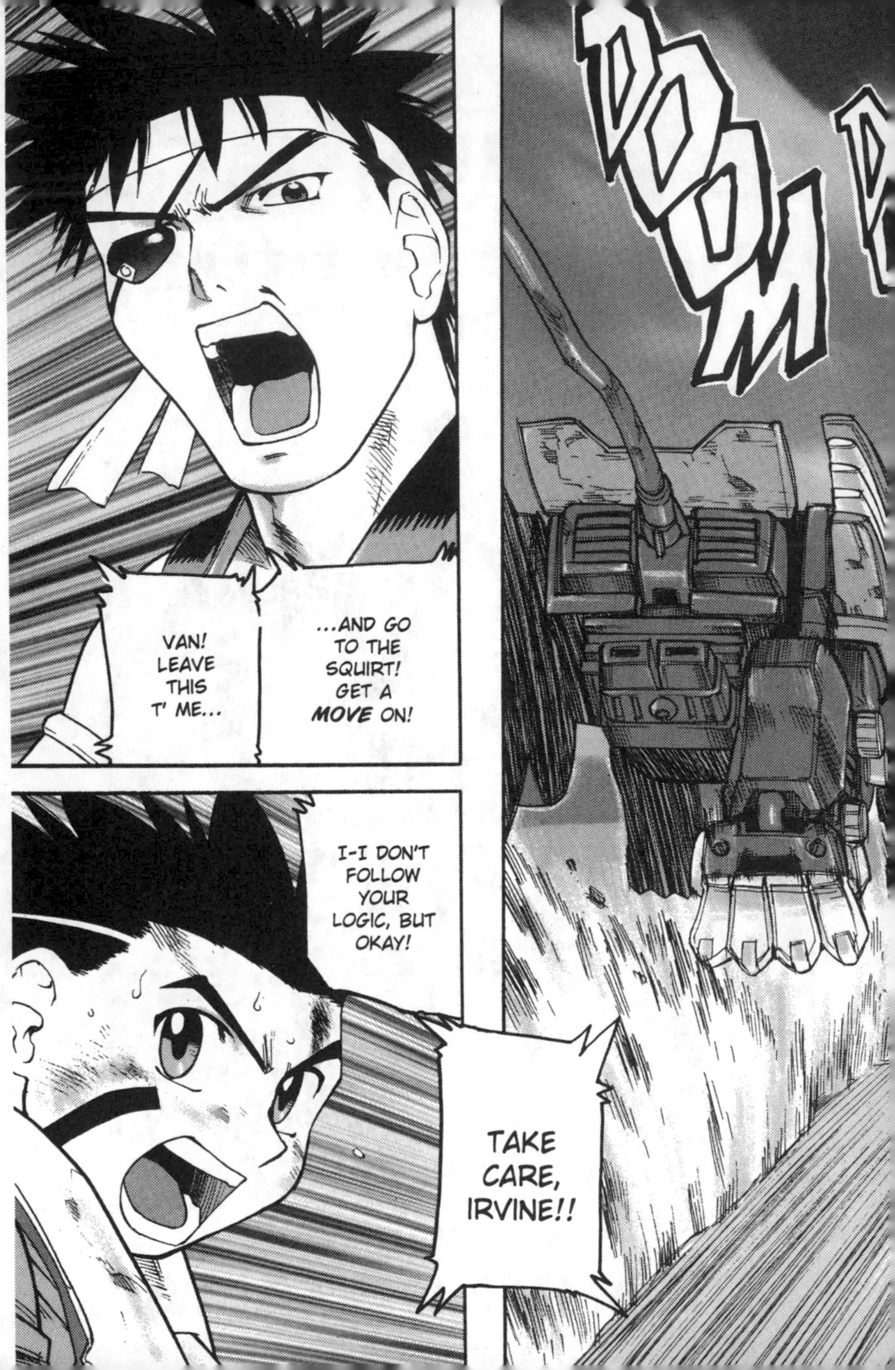
VAN! LEAVE THIS T' ME...
...AND GO TO THE SQUIRT! GET A *MOVE* ON!
I-I DON'T FOLLOW YOUR LOGIC, BUT OKAY!
TAKE CARE, IRVINE!!
DOOM

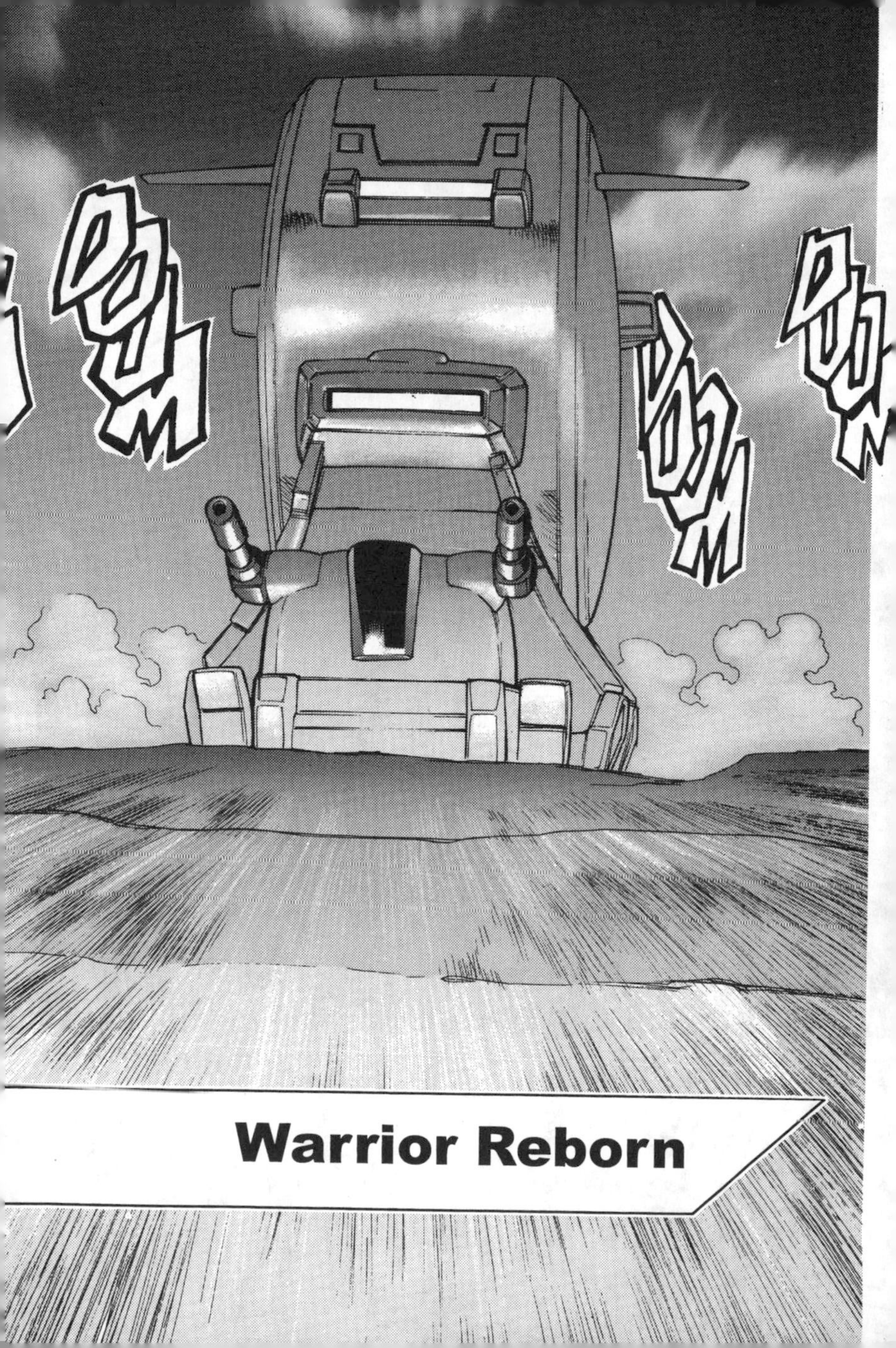
DOOM
DOOM

Warrior Reborn

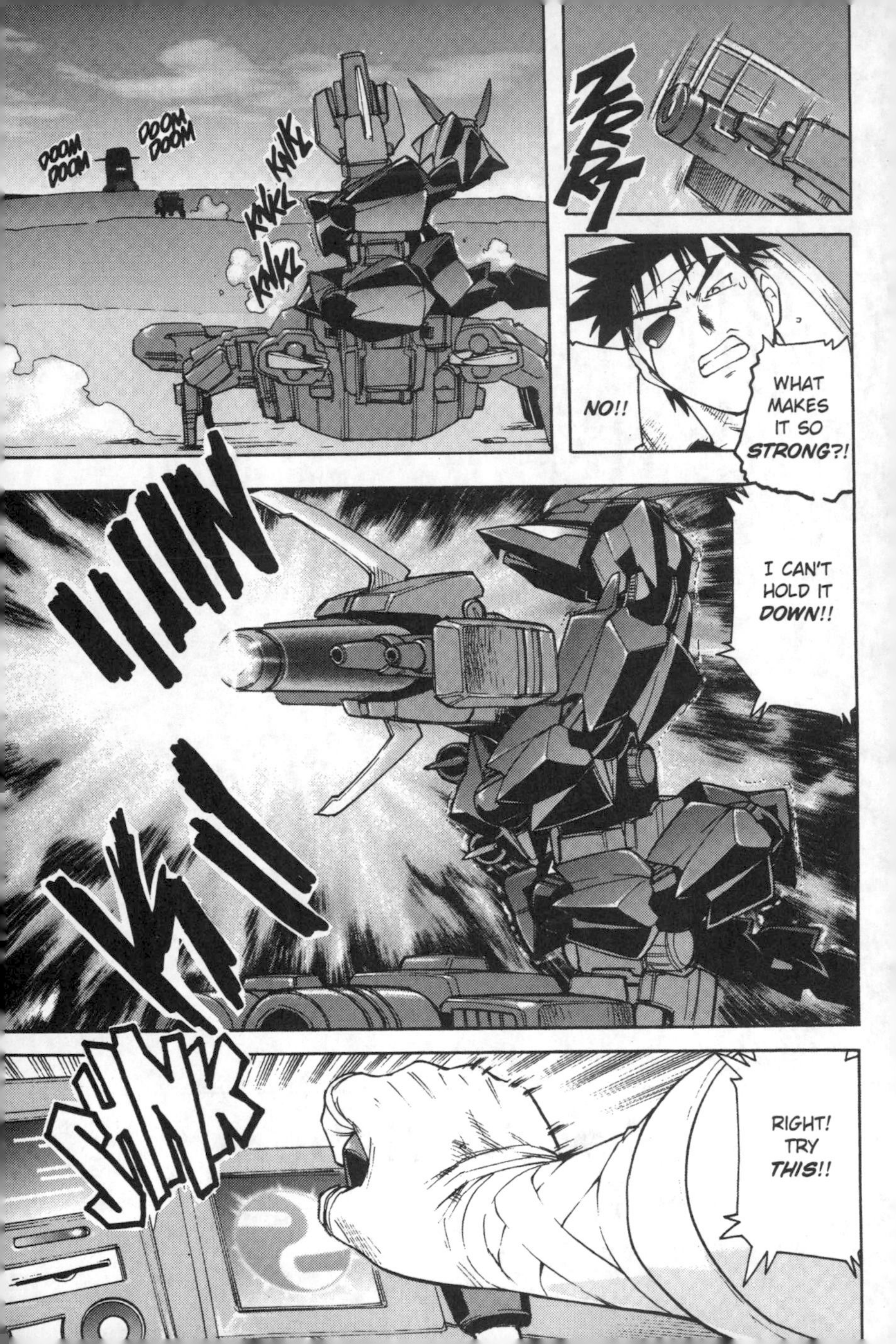
DOOM DOOM
DOOM DOOM
KNKL KNKL
KNKL
KNKL
ZRRT
NO!!
WHAT MAKES IT SO STRONG?!
WHIN
I CAN'T HOLD IT DOWN!!
CHAK
RIGHT! TRY THIS!!

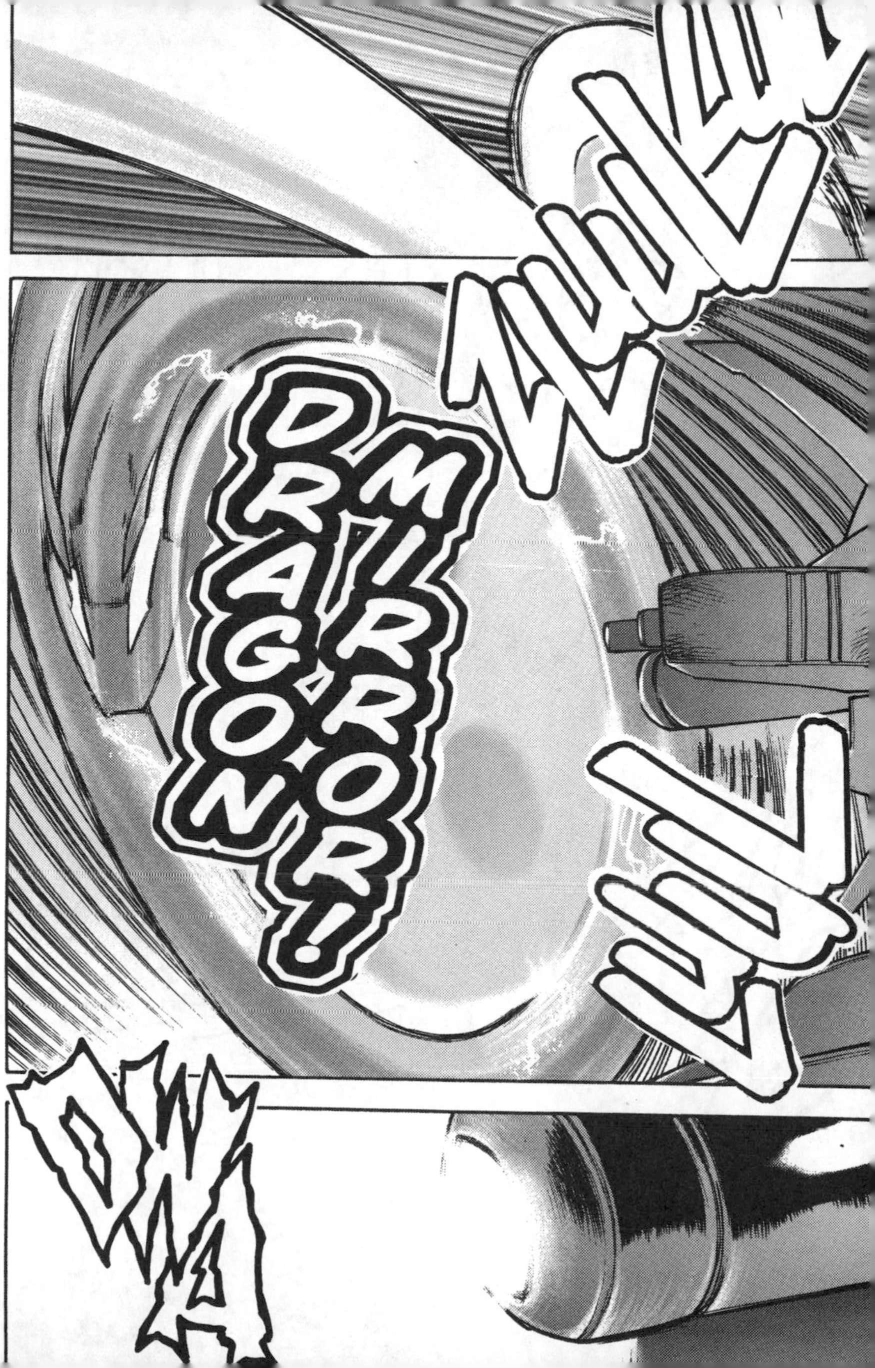
DRAGON MIRROR!

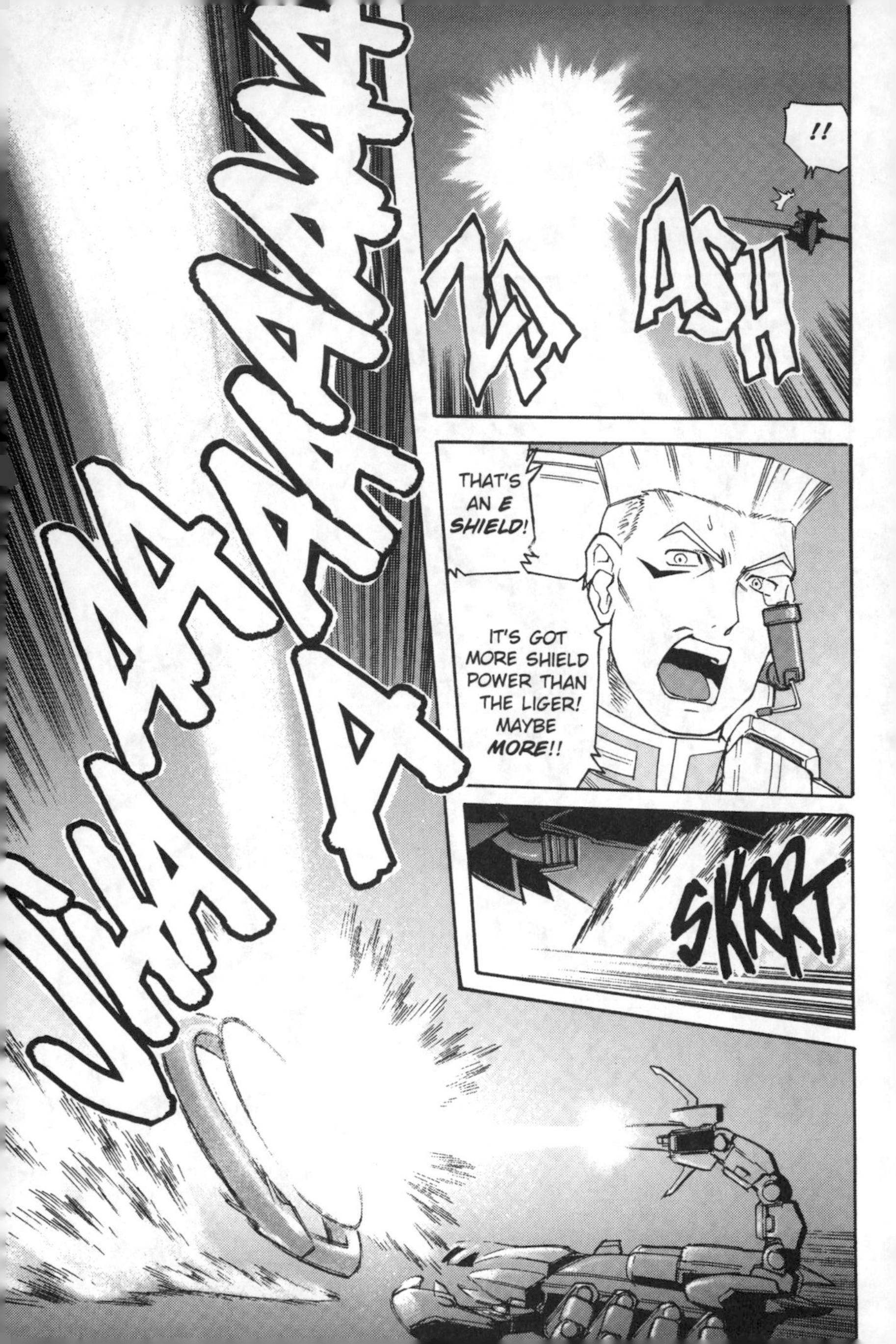
!!
ZA ASH
THAT'S AN *E SHIELD*!
IT'S GOT MORE SHIELD POWER THAN THE LIGER! MAYBE *MORE*!!
SKRRT

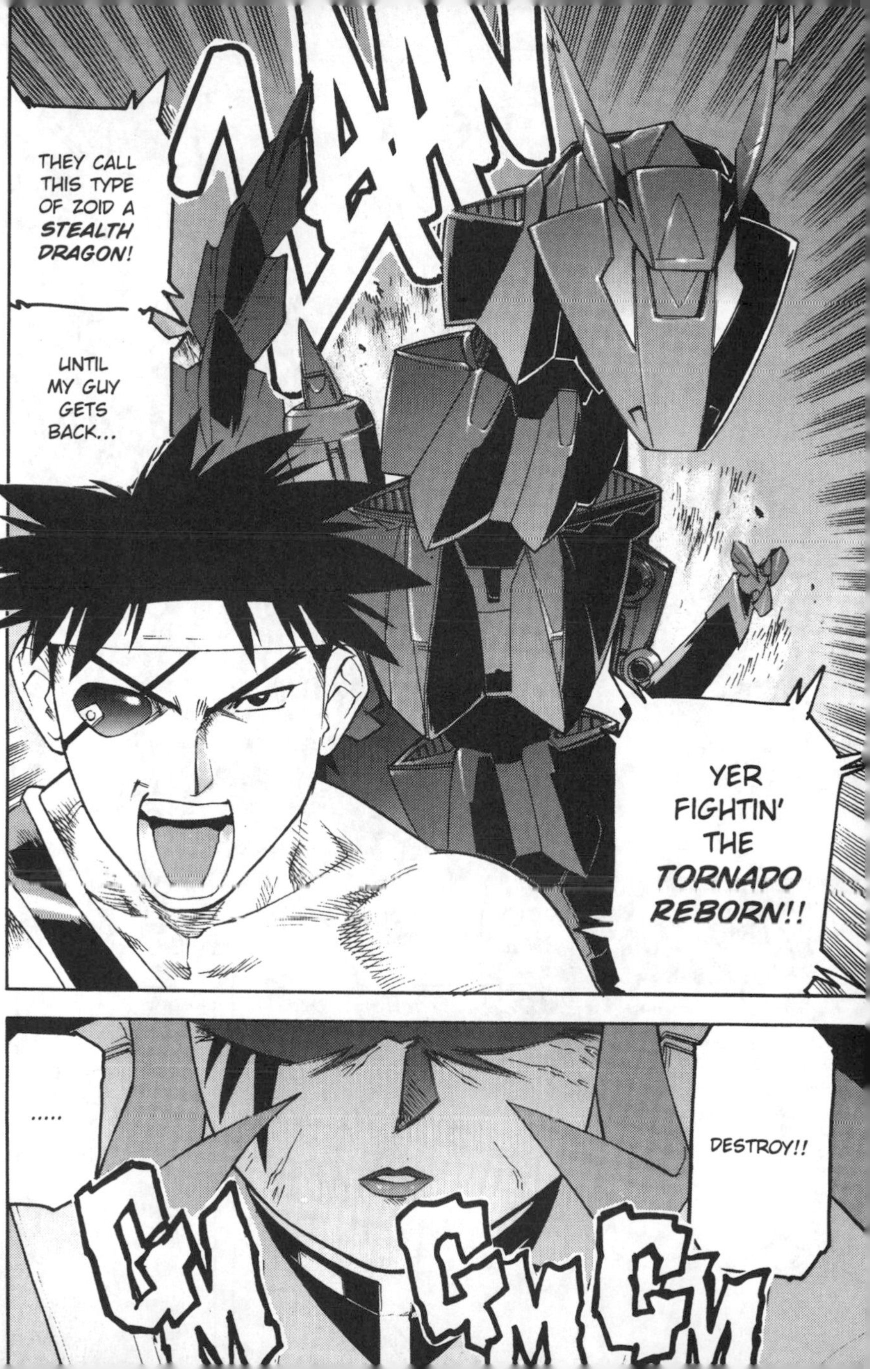
THEY CALL THIS TYPE OF ZOID A *STEALTH DRAGON!*
UNTIL MY GUY GETS BACK...
YER FIGHTIN' THE *TORNADO REBORN!!*
.....
DESTROY!!

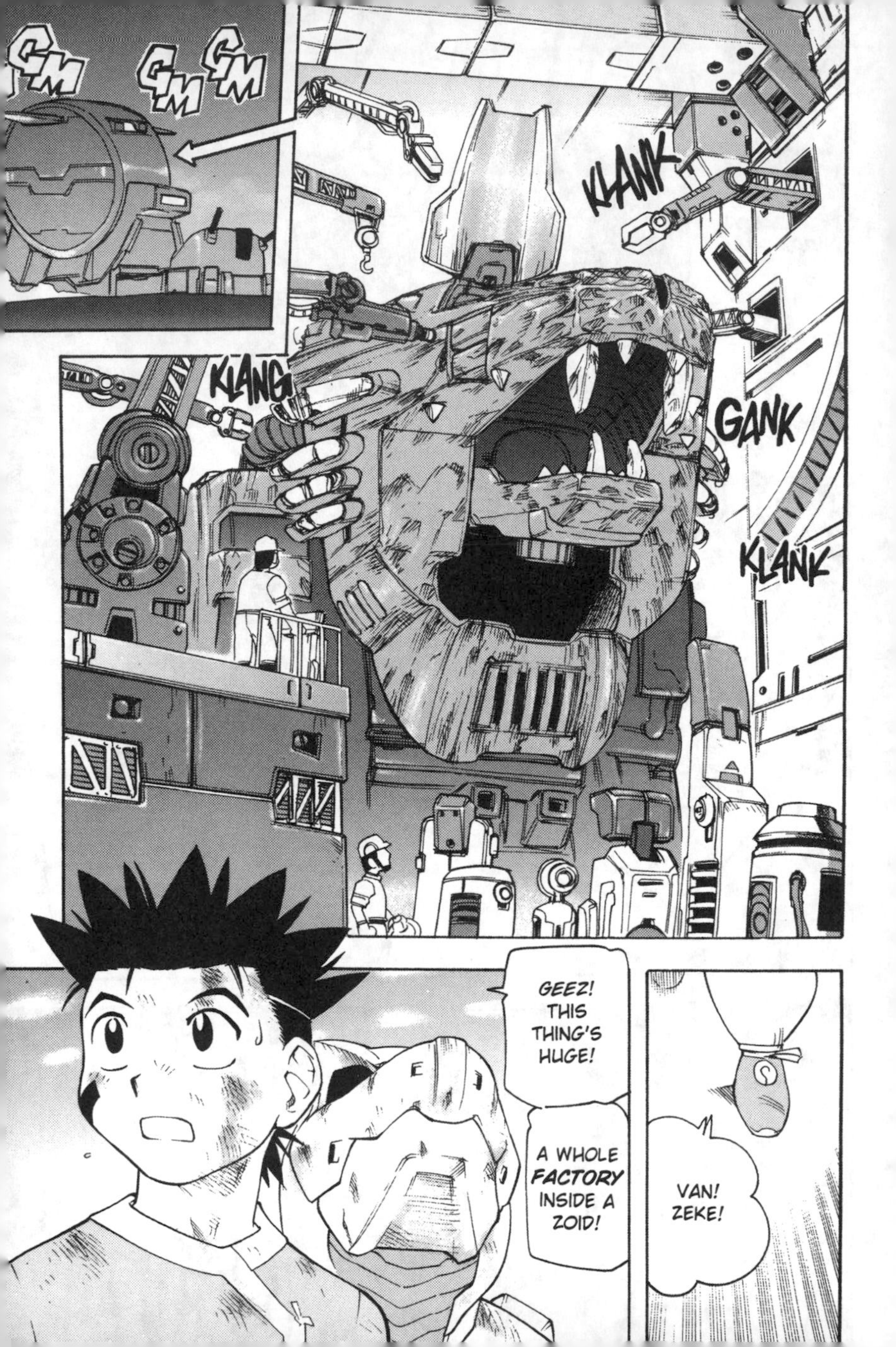

GM
GM
GM
KLANK
KLANG
GANK
KLANK
GEEZ! THIS THING'S HUGE!
A WHOLE **FACTORY** INSIDE A ZOID!
VAN! ZEKE!

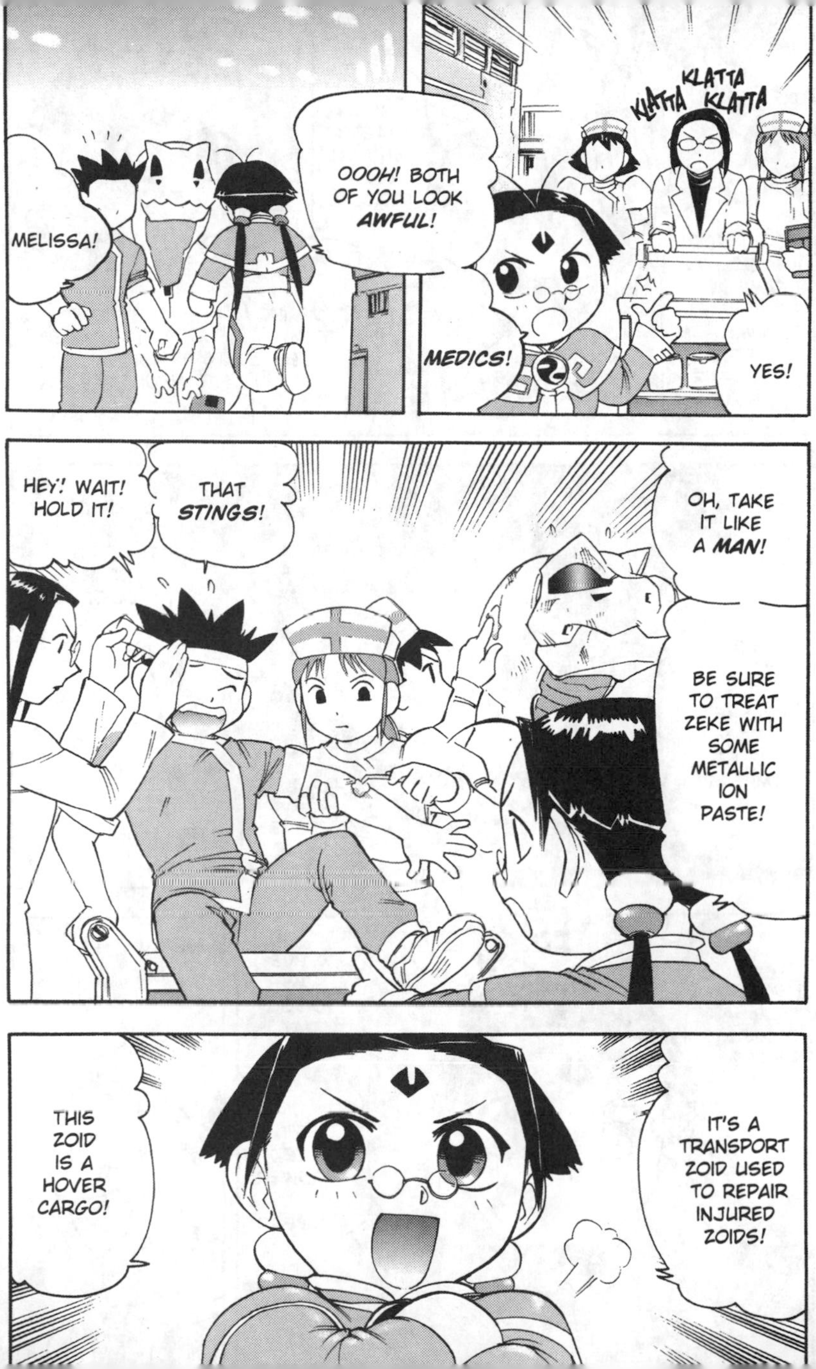

MELISSA!
OOOH! BOTH OF YOU LOOK AWFUL!
KLATTA KLATTA KLATTA
MEDICS!
YES!
HEY! WAIT! HOLD IT!
THAT STINGS!
OH, TAKE IT LIKE A MAN!
BE SURE TO TREAT ZEKE WITH SOME METALLIC ION PASTE!
THIS ZOID IS A HOVER CARGO!
IT'S A TRANSPORT ZOID USED TO REPAIR INJURED ZOIDS!

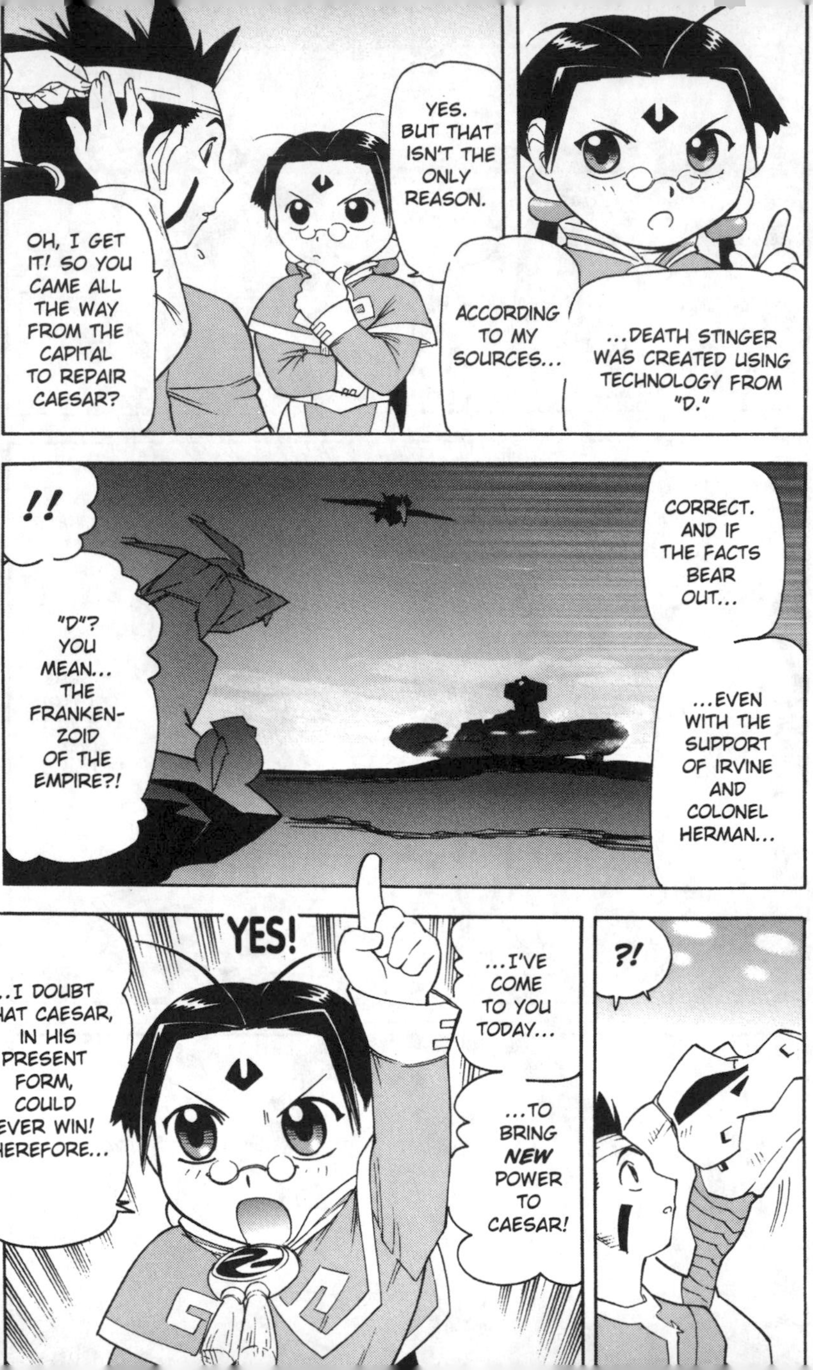
OH, I GET IT! SO YOU CAME ALL THE WAY FROM THE CAPITAL TO REPAIR CAESAR?
YES. BUT THAT ISN'T THE ONLY REASON.
ACCORDING TO MY SOURCES...
...DEATH STINGER WAS CREATED USING TECHNOLOGY FROM "D."
!!
"D"? YOU MEAN... THE FRANKEN-ZOID OF THE EMPIRE?!
CORRECT. AND IF THE FACTS BEAR OUT...
...EVEN WITH THE SUPPORT OF IRVINE AND COLONEL HERMAN...
...I DOUBT THAT CAESAR, IN HIS PRESENT FORM, COULD EVER WIN! THEREFORE...
YES!
...I'VE COME TO YOU TODAY...
...TO BRING *NEW* POWER TO CAESAR!
?!

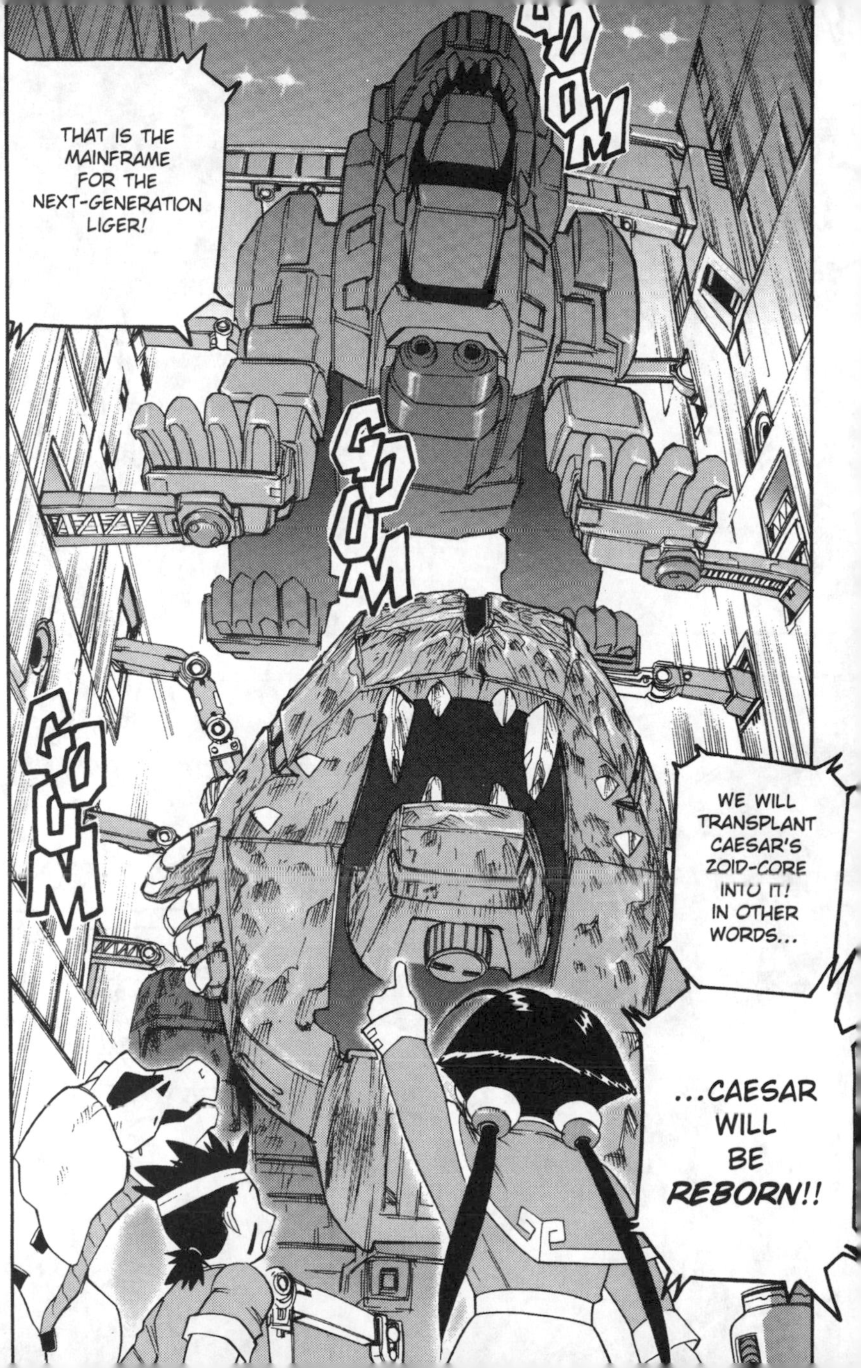
GOOM
THAT IS THE MAINFRAME FOR THE NEXT-GENERATION LIGER!
GOOM
GOOM
WE WILL TRANSPLANT CAESAR'S ZOID-CORE INTO IT! IN OTHER WORDS...
...CAESAR WILL BE REBORN!!

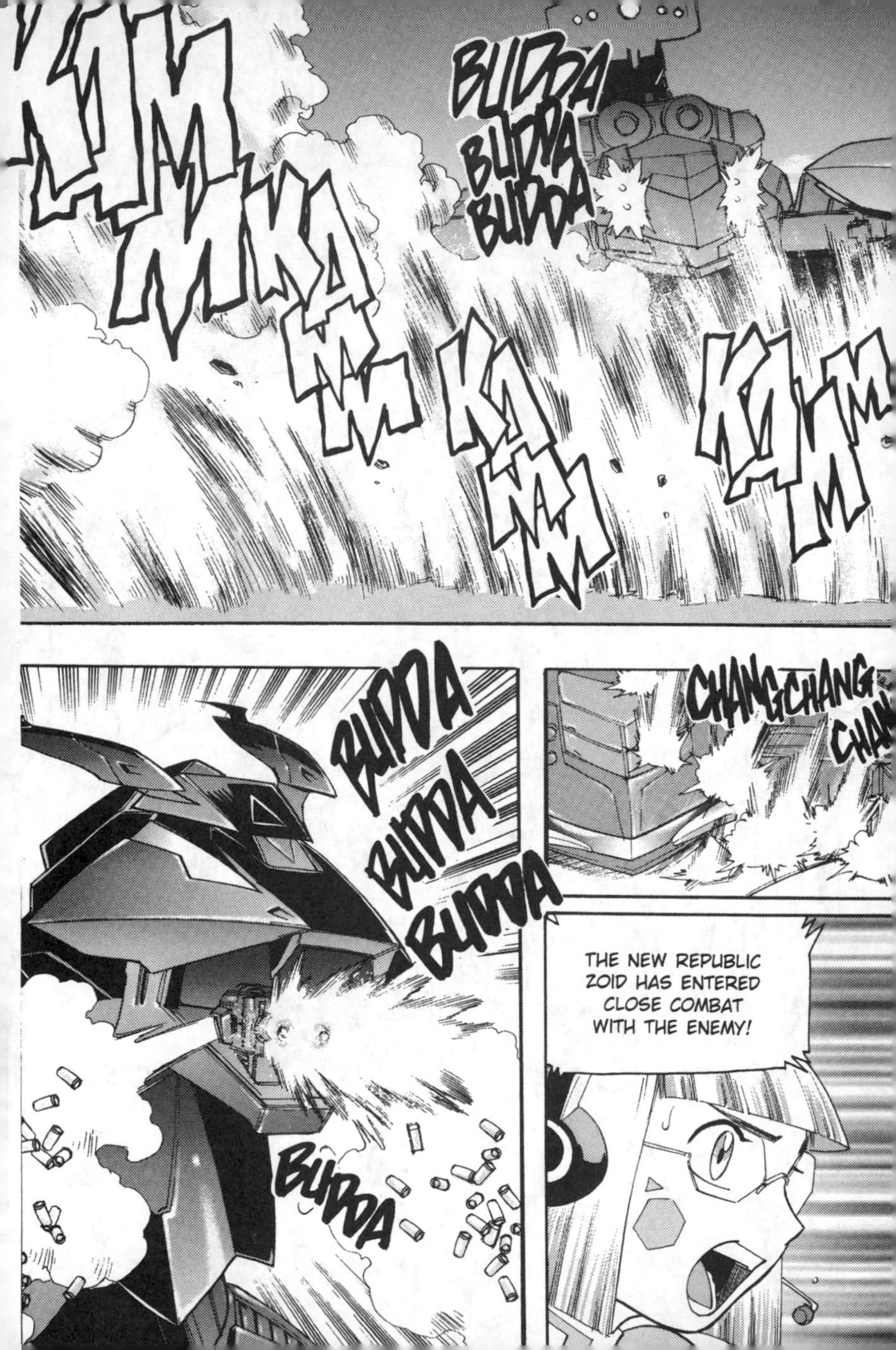
BUDDA BUDDA BUDDA
BUDDA BUDDA BUDDA
BUDDA
CHANGCHANG
CHAN
THE NEW REPUBLIC ZOID HAS ENTERED CLOSE COMBAT WITH THE ENEMY!

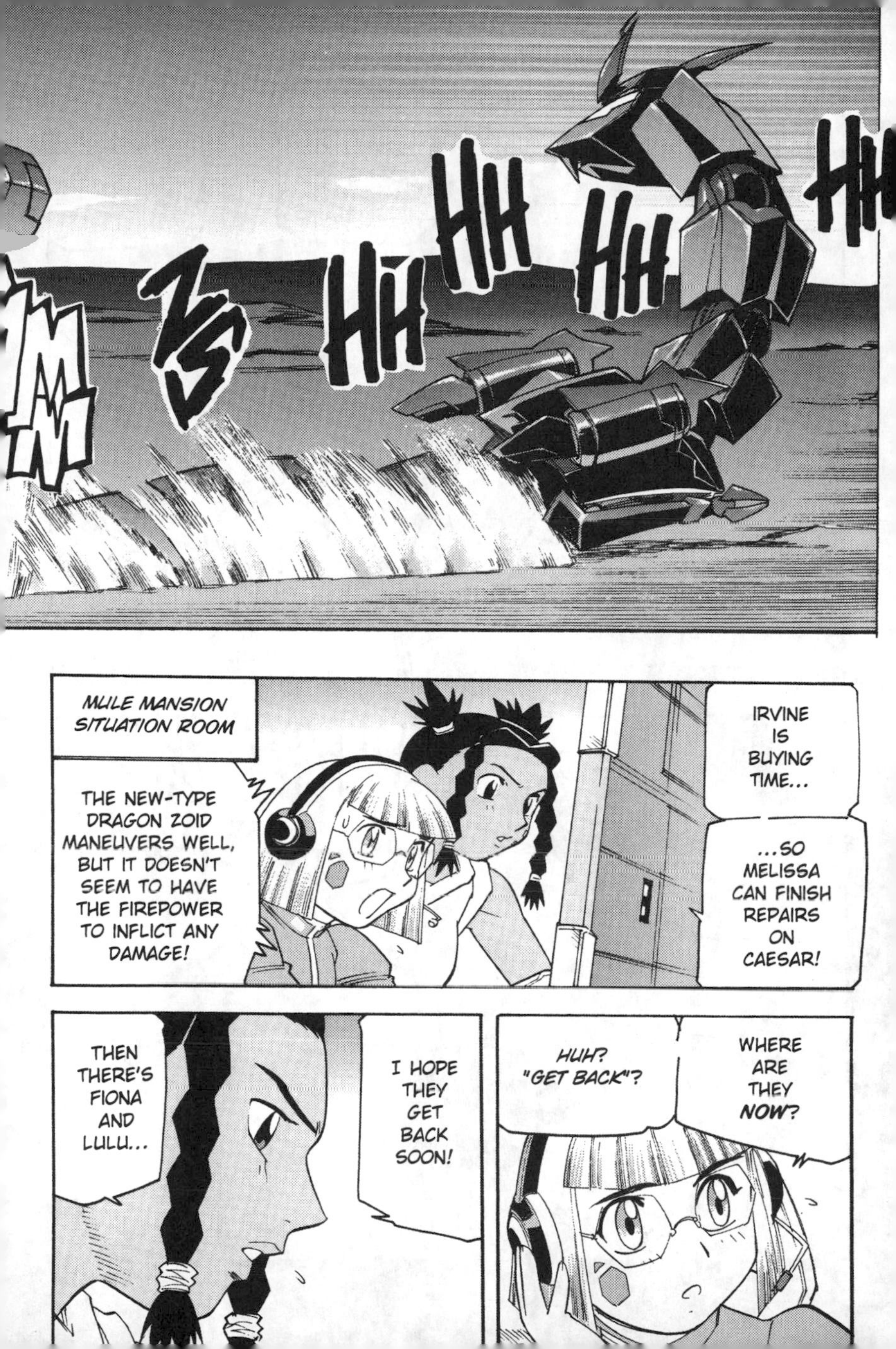
ZSHHHHHHHH
MULE MANSION SITUATION ROOM
THE NEW-TYPE DRAGON ZOID MANEUVERS WELL, BUT IT DOESN'T SEEM TO HAVE THE FIREPOWER TO INFLICT ANY DAMAGE!
IRVINE IS BUYING TIME...
...SO MELISSA CAN FINISH REPAIRS ON CAESAR!
THEN THERE'S FIONA AND LULU...
I HOPE THEY GET BACK SOON!
HUH? "GET BACK"?
WHERE ARE THEY *NOW*?

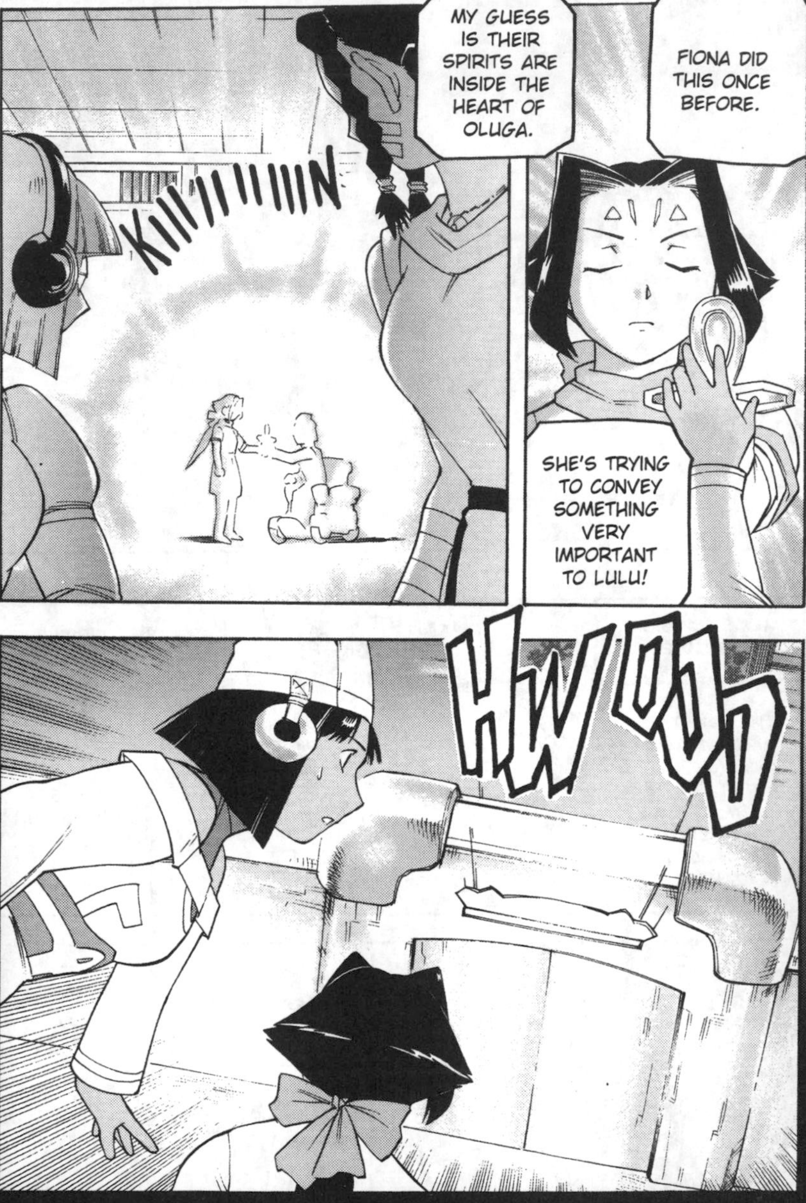
MY GUESS IS THEIR SPIRITS ARE INSIDE THE HEART OF OLUGA.
KIIIIIIIIN
FIONA DID THIS ONCE BEFORE.
SHE'S TRYING TO CONVEY SOMETHING VERY IMPORTANT TO LULU!
HWOOO

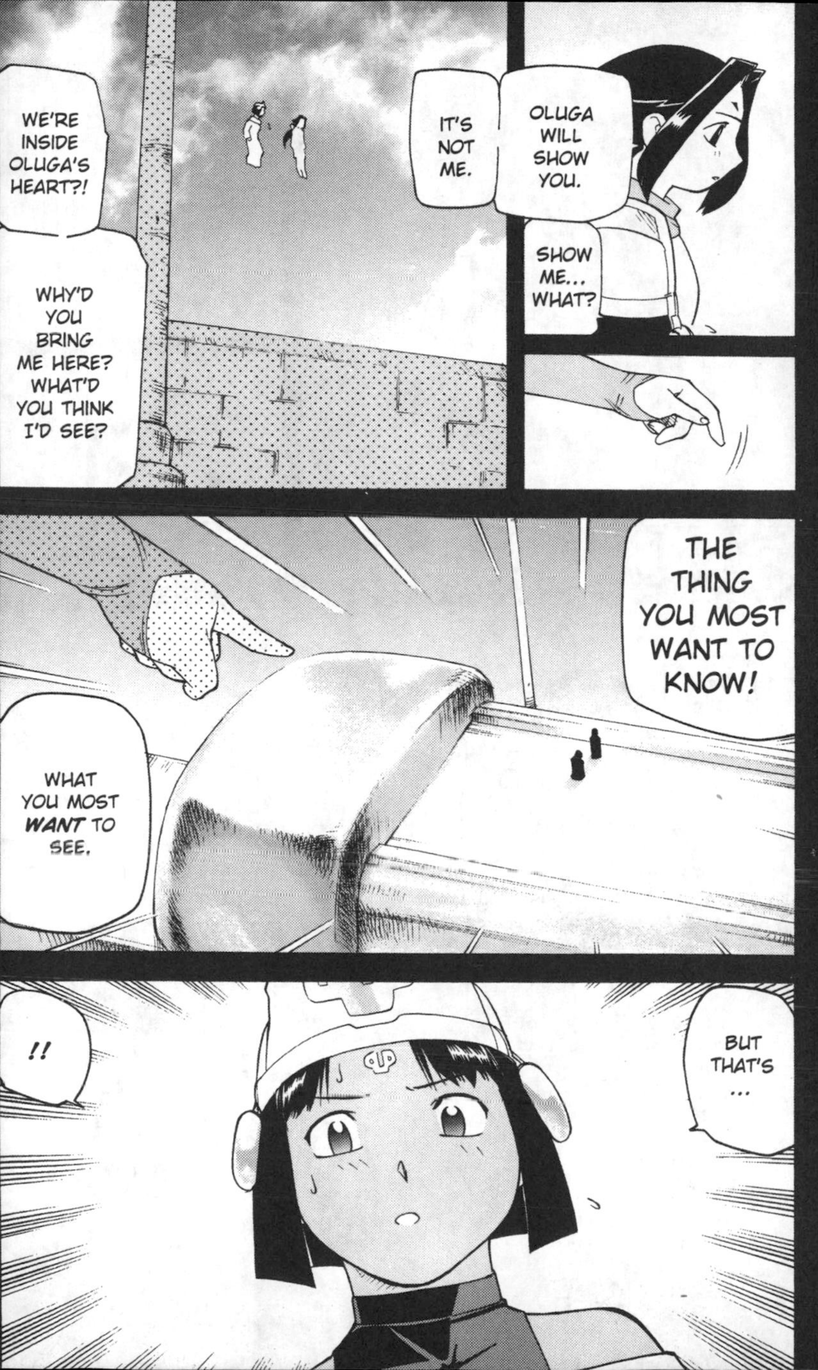
WE'RE INSIDE OLUGA'S HEART?!
WHY'D YOU BRING ME HERE? WHAT'D YOU THINK I'D SEE?
IT'S NOT ME.
OLUGA WILL SHOW YOU.
SHOW ME... WHAT?
THE THING YOU MOST WANT TO KNOW!
WHAT YOU MOST *WANT* TO SEE.
!!
BUT THAT'S ...

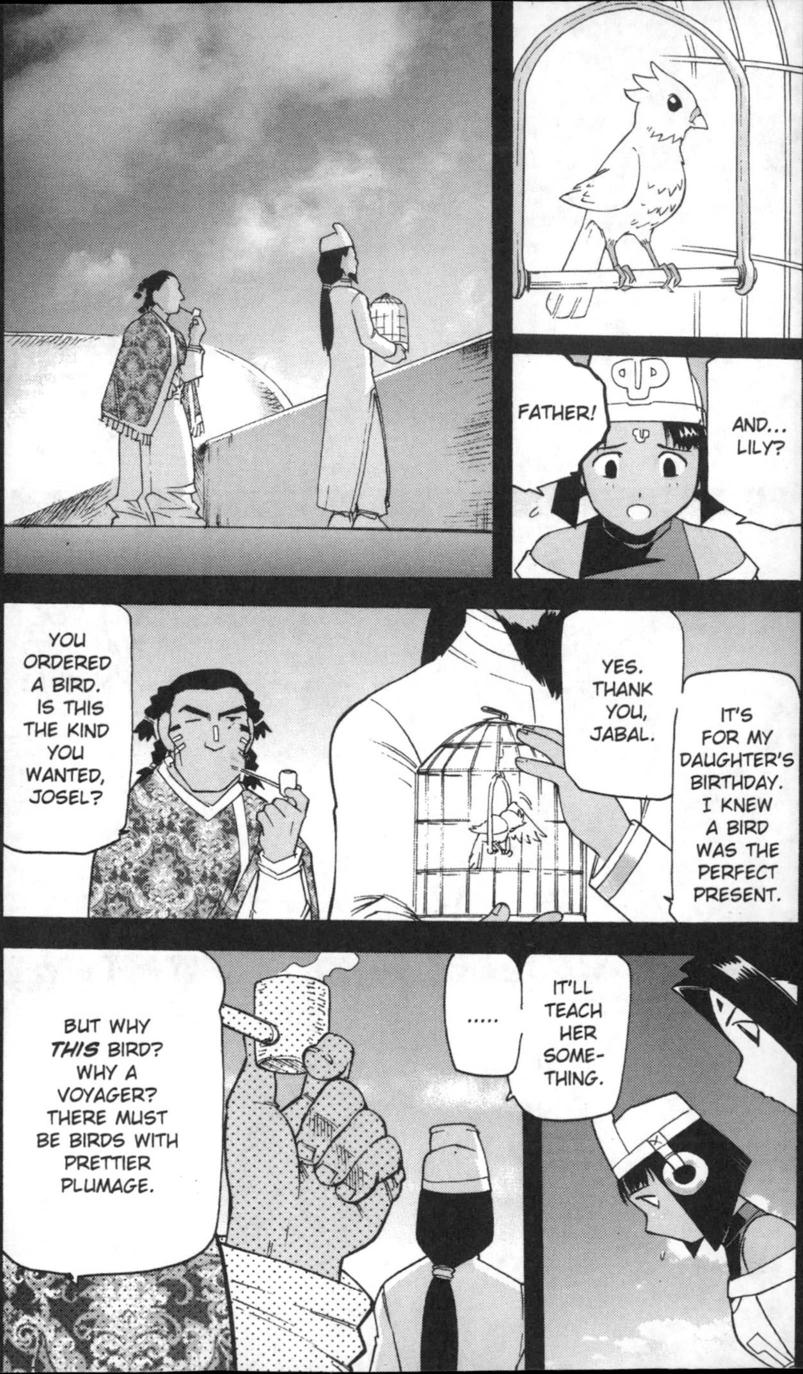
FATHER!
AND... LILY?
YOU ORDERED A BIRD. IS THIS THE KIND YOU WANTED, JOSEL?
YES. THANK YOU, JABAL.
IT'S FOR MY DAUGHTER'S BIRTHDAY. I KNEW A BIRD WAS THE PERFECT PRESENT.
BUT WHY *THIS* BIRD? WHY A VOYAGER? THERE MUST BE BIRDS WITH PRETTIER PLUMAGE.
.....
IT'LL TEACH HER SOMETHING.

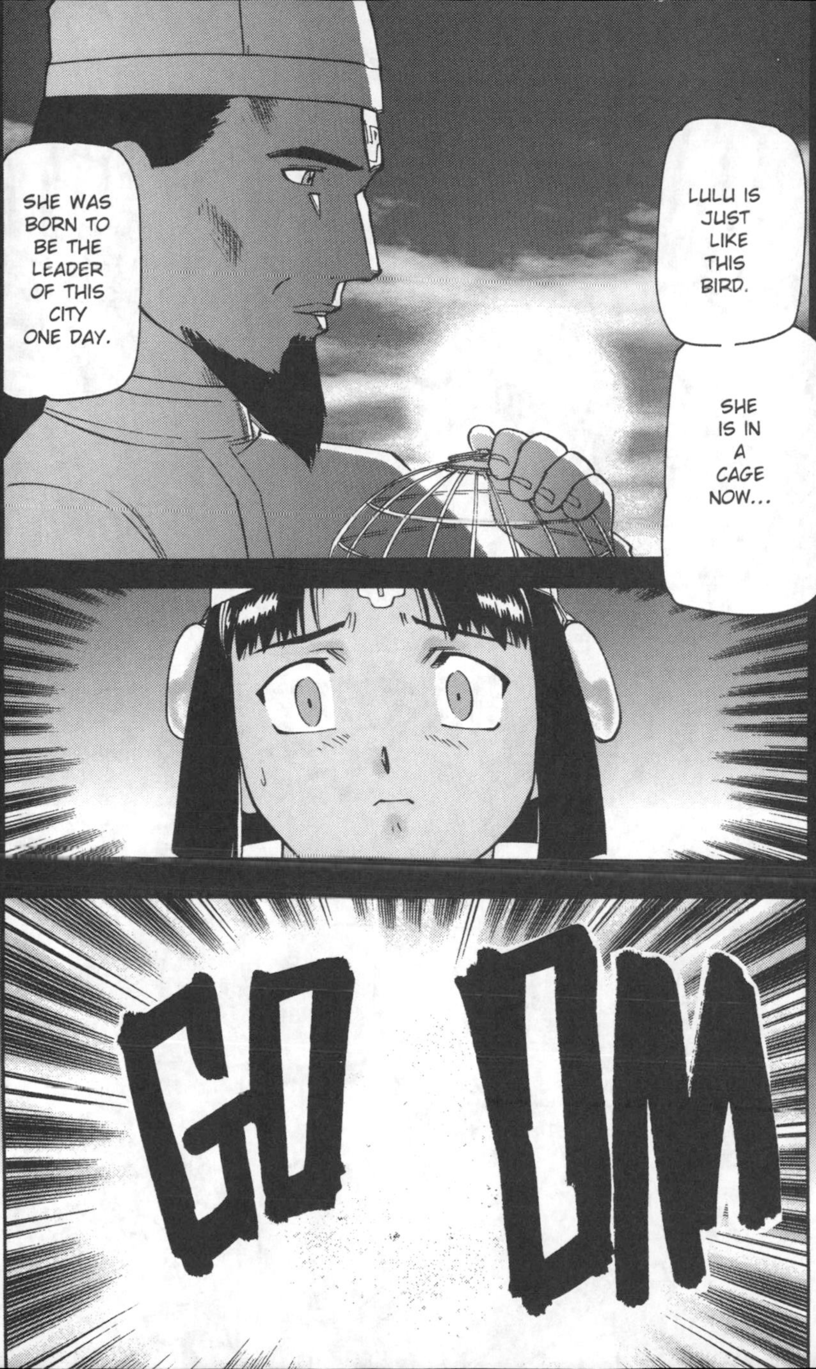
SHE WAS BORN TO BE THE LEADER OF THIS CITY ONE DAY.
LULU IS JUST LIKE THIS BIRD.
SHE IS IN A CAGE NOW...
GOOM

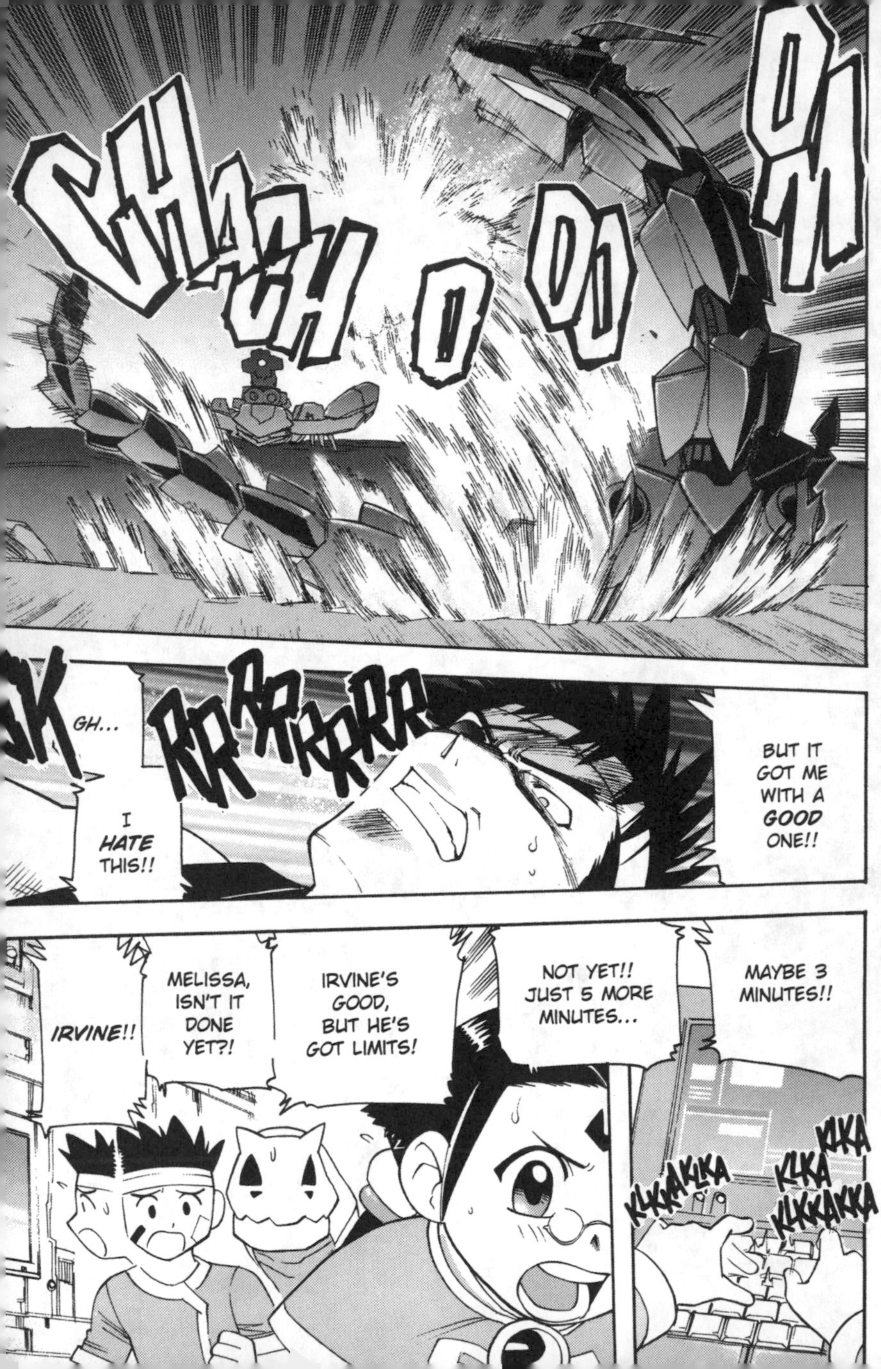
GH...
I *HATE* THIS!!
BUT IT GOT ME WITH A *GOOD* ONE!!
IRVINE!!
MELISSA, ISN'T IT DONE YET?!
IRVINE'S GOOD, BUT HE'S GOT LIMITS!
NOT YET!! JUST 5 MORE MINUTES...
MAYBE 3 MINUTES!!

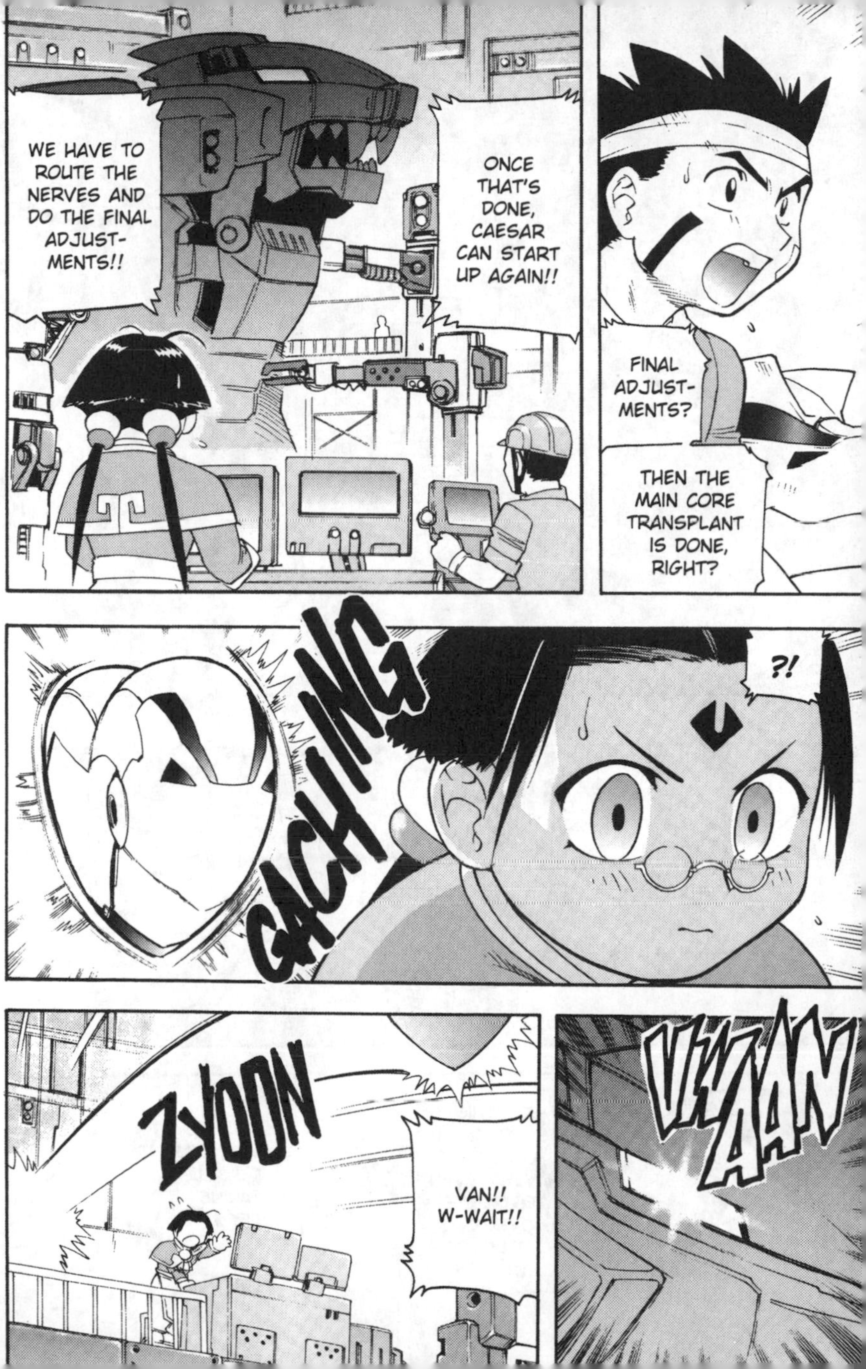
WE HAVE TO ROUTE THE NERVES AND DO THE FINAL ADJUST-MENTS!!
ONCE THAT'S DONE, CAESAR CAN START UP AGAIN!!
FINAL ADJUST-MENTS?
THEN THE MAIN CORE TRANSPLANT IS DONE, RIGHT?
GACHING
?!
ZYOON
VAN!! W-WAIT!!
VWAAN

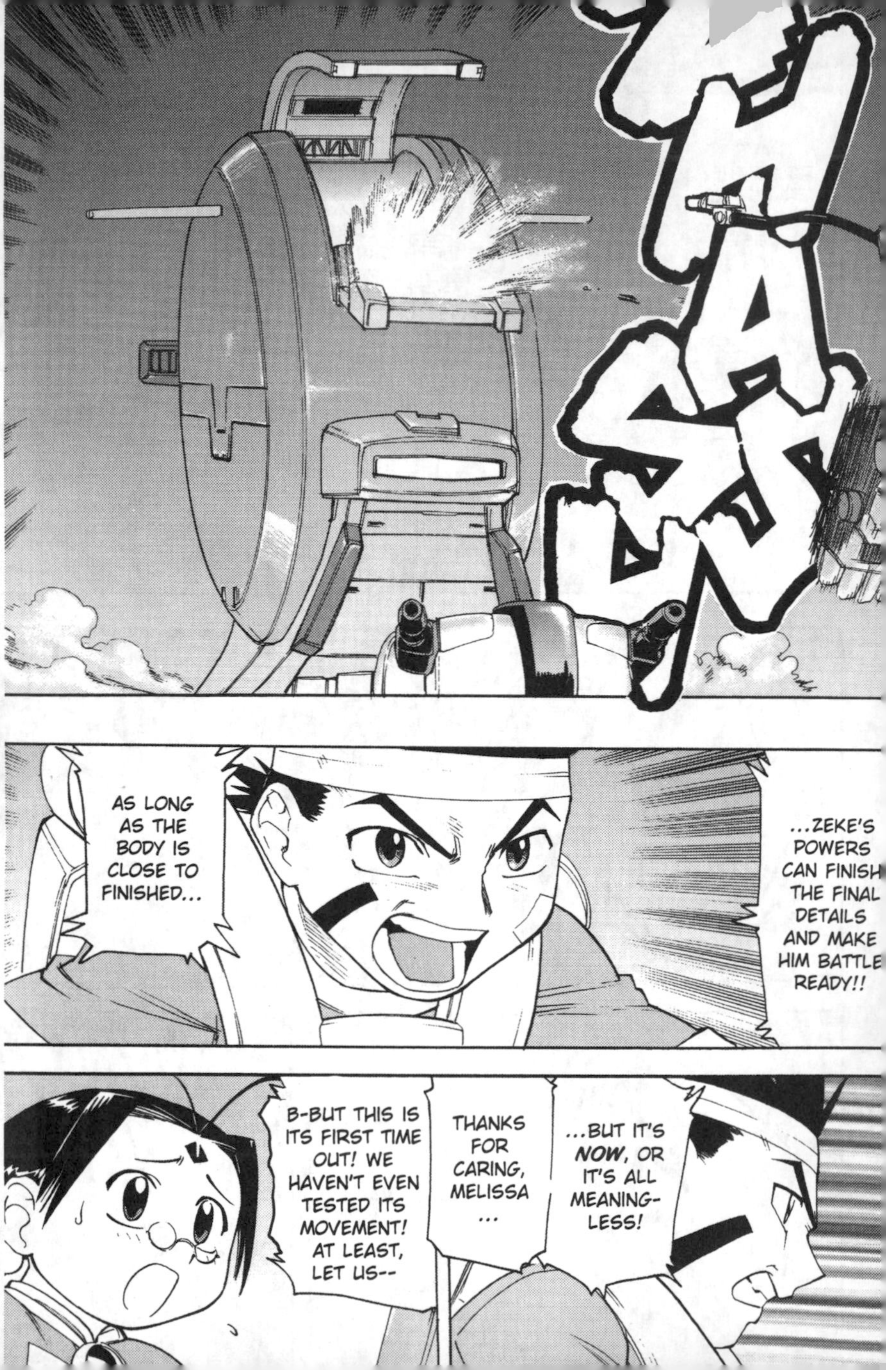
AS LONG AS THE BODY IS CLOSE TO FINISHED...
...ZEKE'S POWERS CAN FINISH THE FINAL DETAILS AND MAKE HIM BATTLE READY!!
B-BUT THIS IS ITS FIRST TIME OUT! WE HAVEN'T EVEN TESTED ITS MOVEMENT! AT LEAST, LET US--
THANKS FOR CARING, MELISSA ...
...BUT IT'S *NOW*, OR IT'S ALL MEANING-LESS!

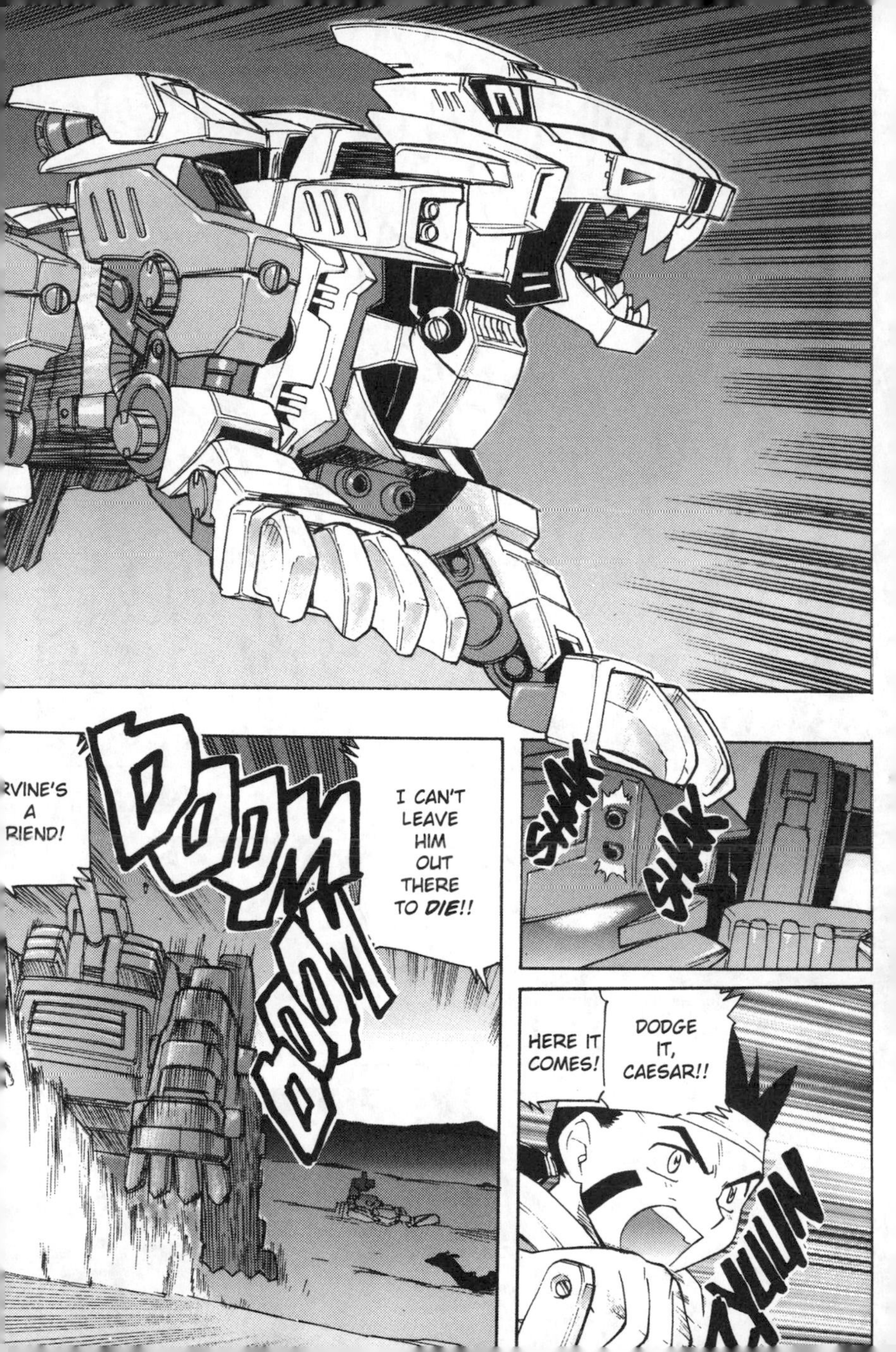
RVINE'S A RIEND!
DOOM
I CAN'T LEAVE HIM OUT THERE TO *DIE*!!
DOOM
SHAK
SHAK
HERE IT COMES!
DODGE IT, CAESAR!!

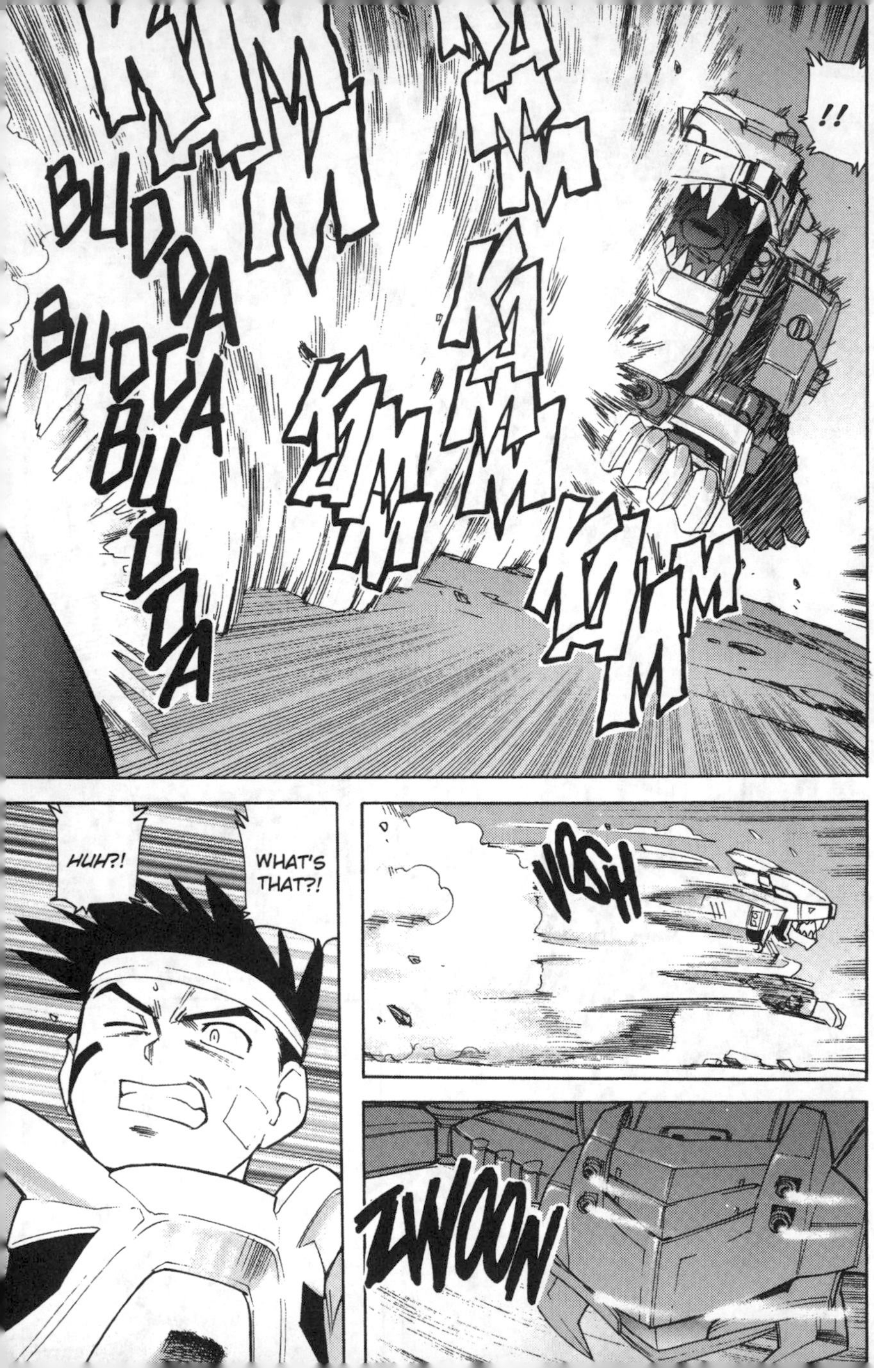
BUDDA
BUDDA
BUDDA
KAMMM
KAMMM
KAMMM
!!
HUH?!
WHAT'S THAT?!
VOSH
ZWOON

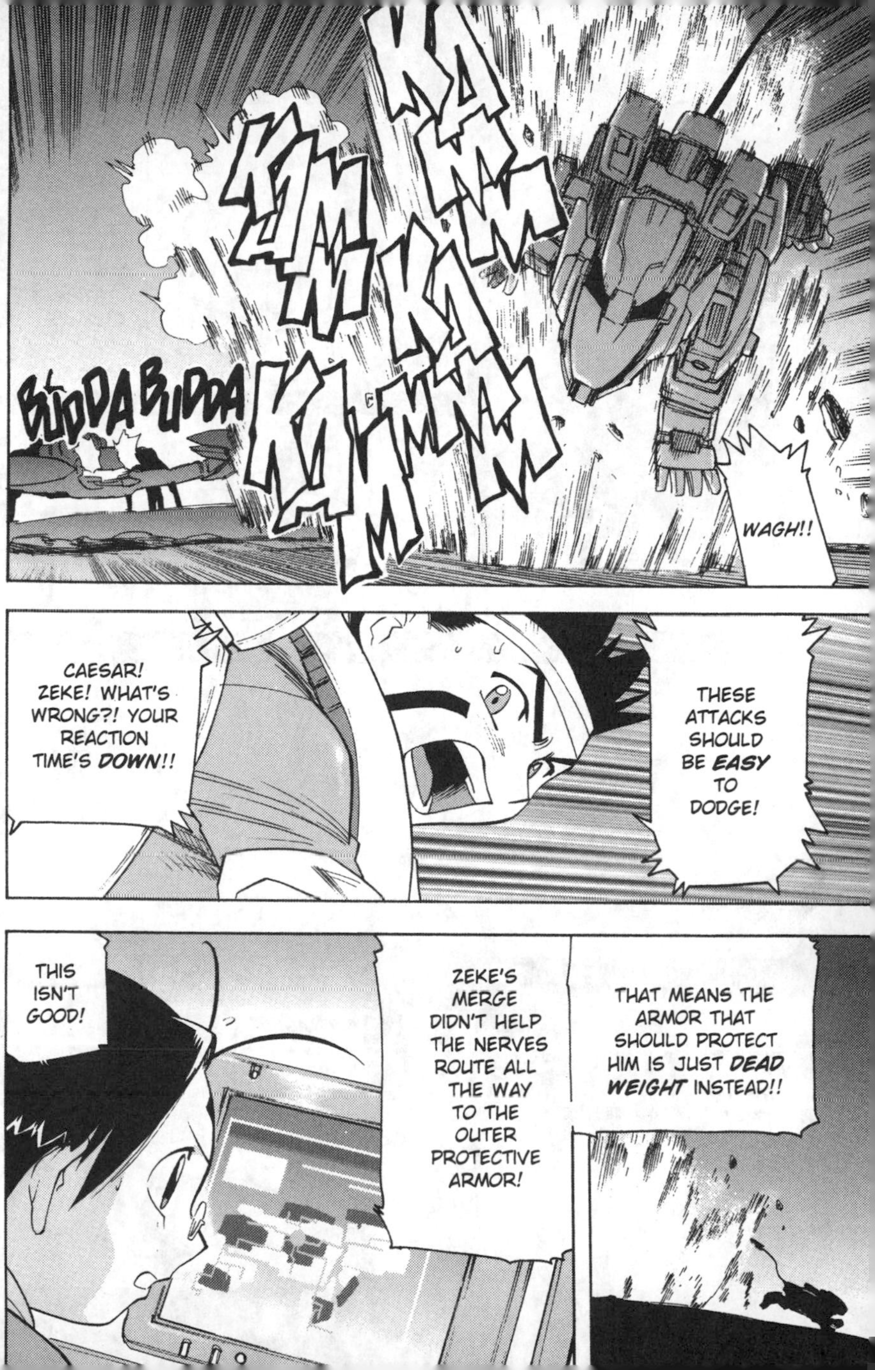
BUDDA BUDDA
WAGH!!
CAESAR! ZEKE! WHAT'S WRONG?! YOUR REACTION TIME'S **DOWN**!!
THESE ATTACKS SHOULD BE **EASY** TO DODGE!
THIS ISN'T GOOD!
ZEKE'S MERGE DIDN'T HELP THE NERVES ROUTE ALL THE WAY TO THE OUTER PROTECTIVE ARMOR!
THAT MEANS THE ARMOR THAT SHOULD PROTECT HIM IS JUST **DEAD WEIGHT** INSTEAD!!

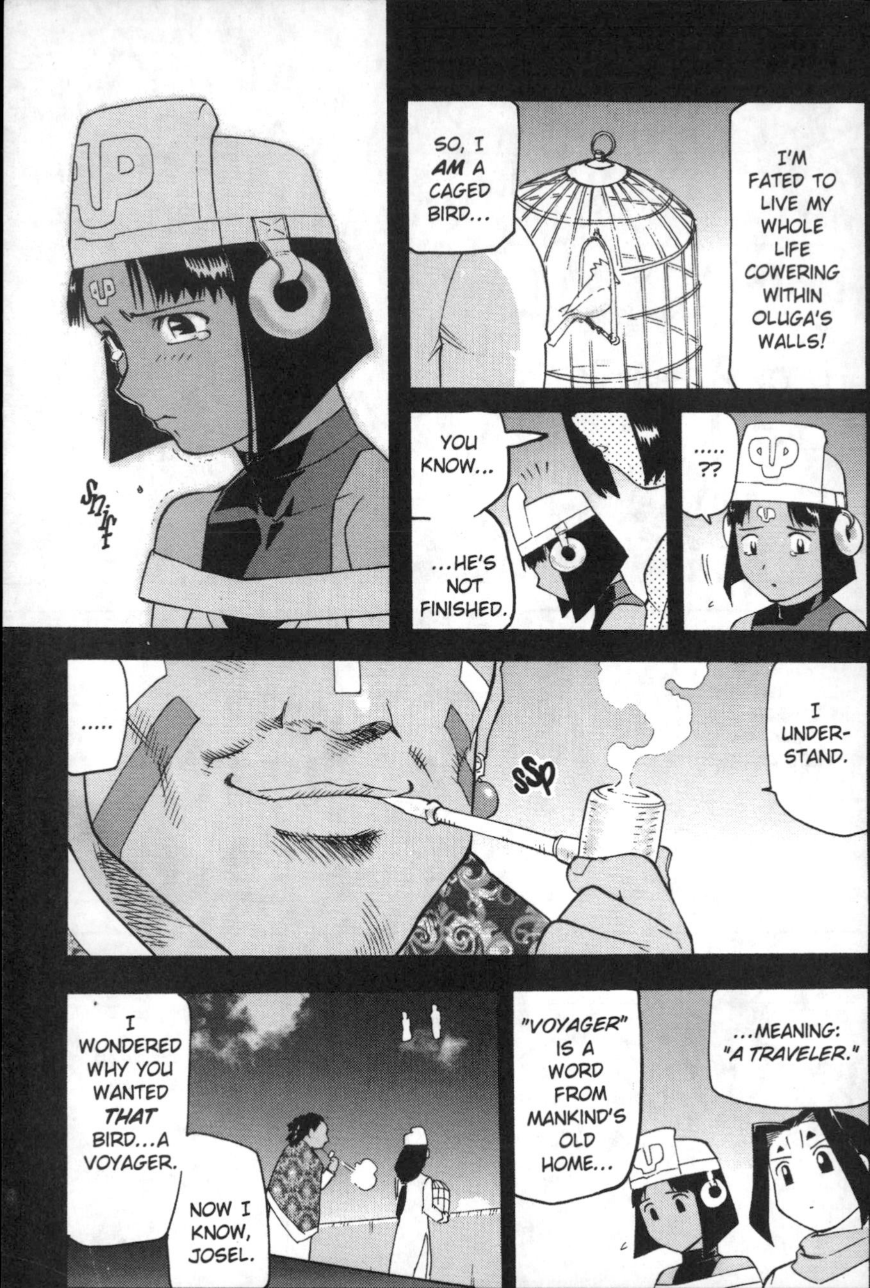
SNIFF
SO, I *AM* A CAGED BIRD...
I'M FATED TO LIVE MY WHOLE LIFE COWERING WITHIN OLUGA'S WALLS!
YOU KNOW...
...HE'S NOT FINISHED.
.....
??
.....
SSP
I UNDERSTAND.
I WONDERED WHY YOU WANTED *THAT* BIRD...A VOYAGER.
NOW I KNOW, JOSEL.
"VOYAGER" IS A WORD FROM MANKIND'S OLD HOME...
...MEANING: "A TRAVELER."

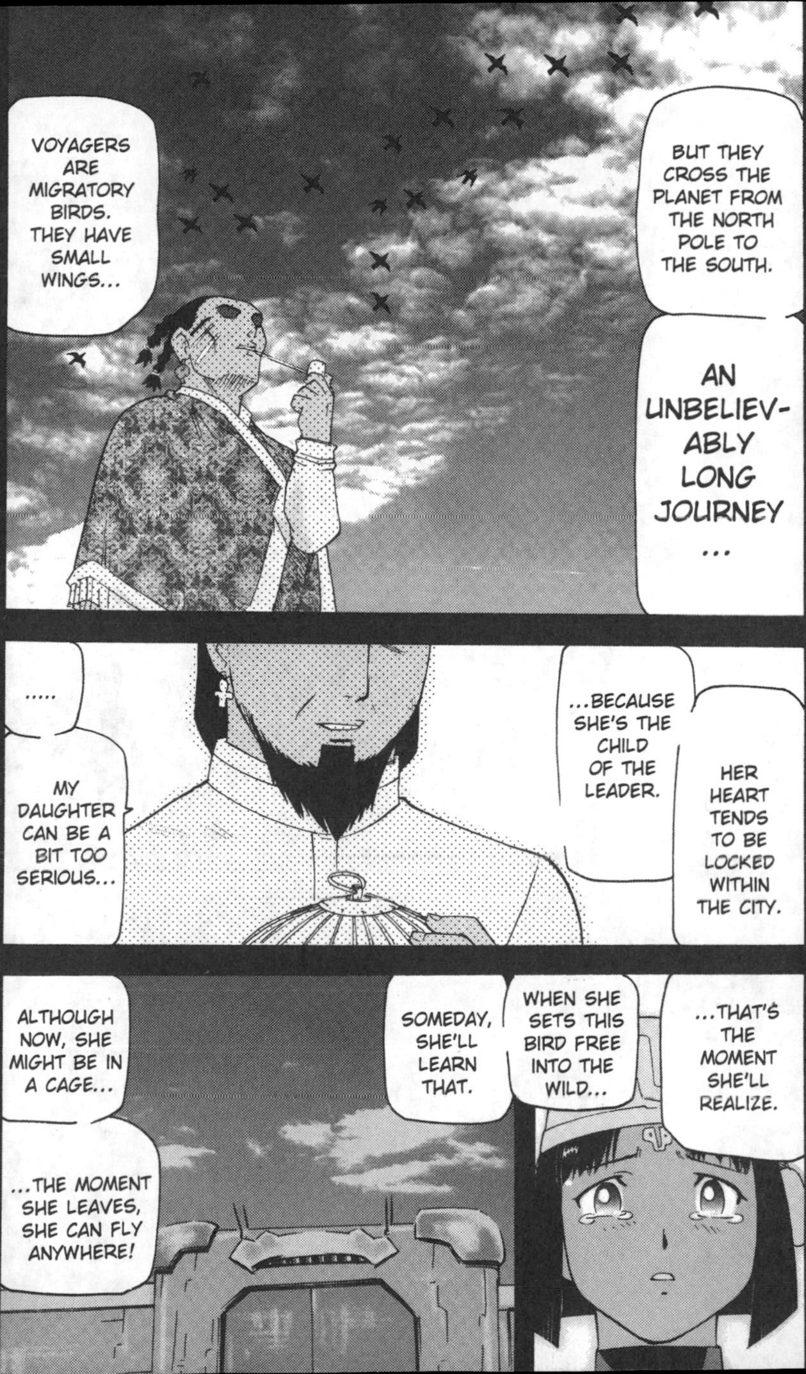
VOYAGERS ARE MIGRATORY BIRDS. THEY HAVE SMALL WINGS...
BUT THEY CROSS THE PLANET FROM THE NORTH POLE TO THE SOUTH.
AN UNBELIEVABLY LONG JOURNEY...
.....
MY DAUGHTER CAN BE A BIT TOO SERIOUS...
...BECAUSE SHE'S THE CHILD OF THE LEADER.
HER HEART TENDS TO BE LOCKED WITHIN THE CITY.
ALTHOUGH NOW, SHE MIGHT BE IN A CAGE...
...THE MOMENT SHE LEAVES, SHE CAN FLY ANYWHERE!
SOMEDAY, SHE'LL LEARN THAT.
WHEN SHE SETS THIS BIRD FREE INTO THE WILD...
...THAT'S THE MOMENT SHE'LL REALIZE.

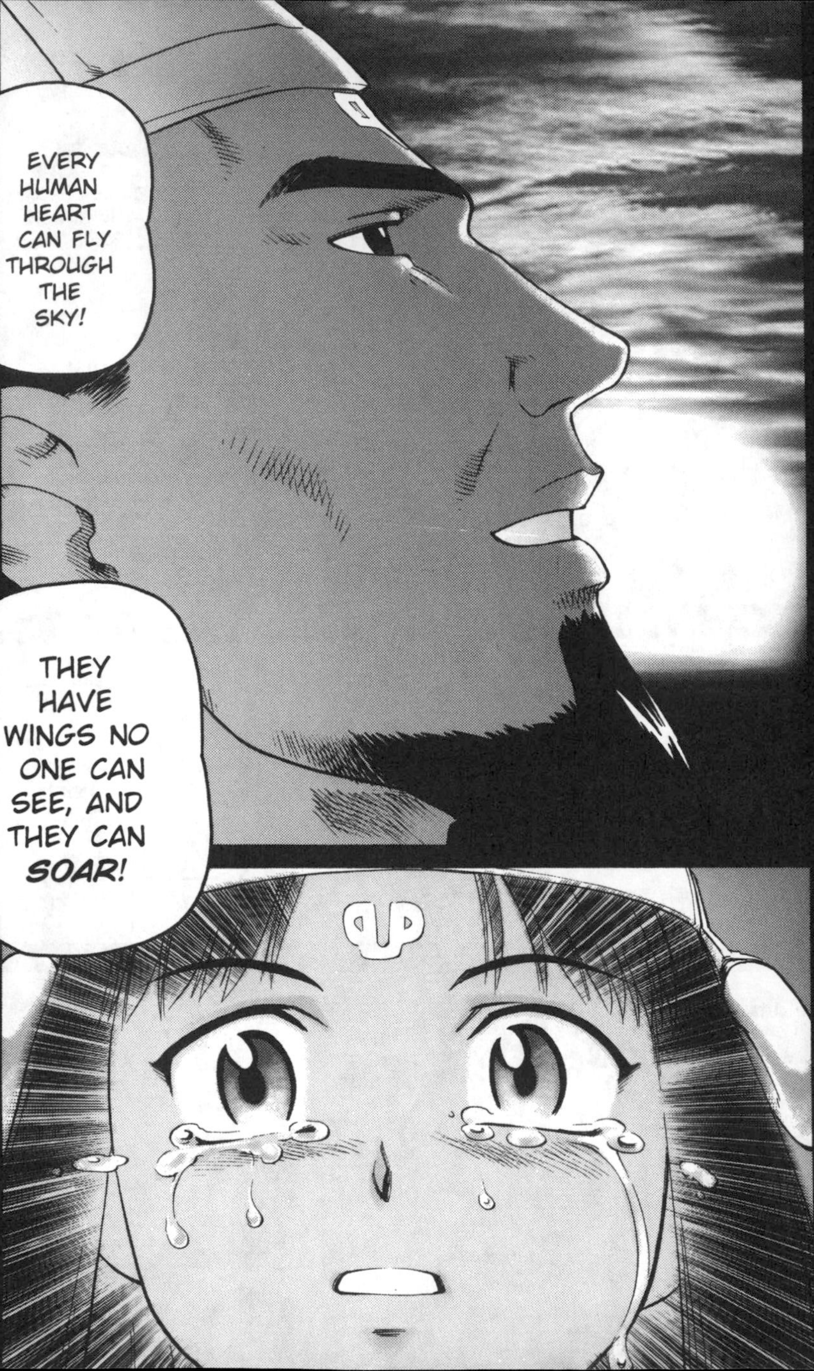
EVERY HUMAN HEART CAN FLY THROUGH THE SKY!
THEY HAVE WINGS NO ONE CAN SEE, AND THEY CAN *SOAR!*

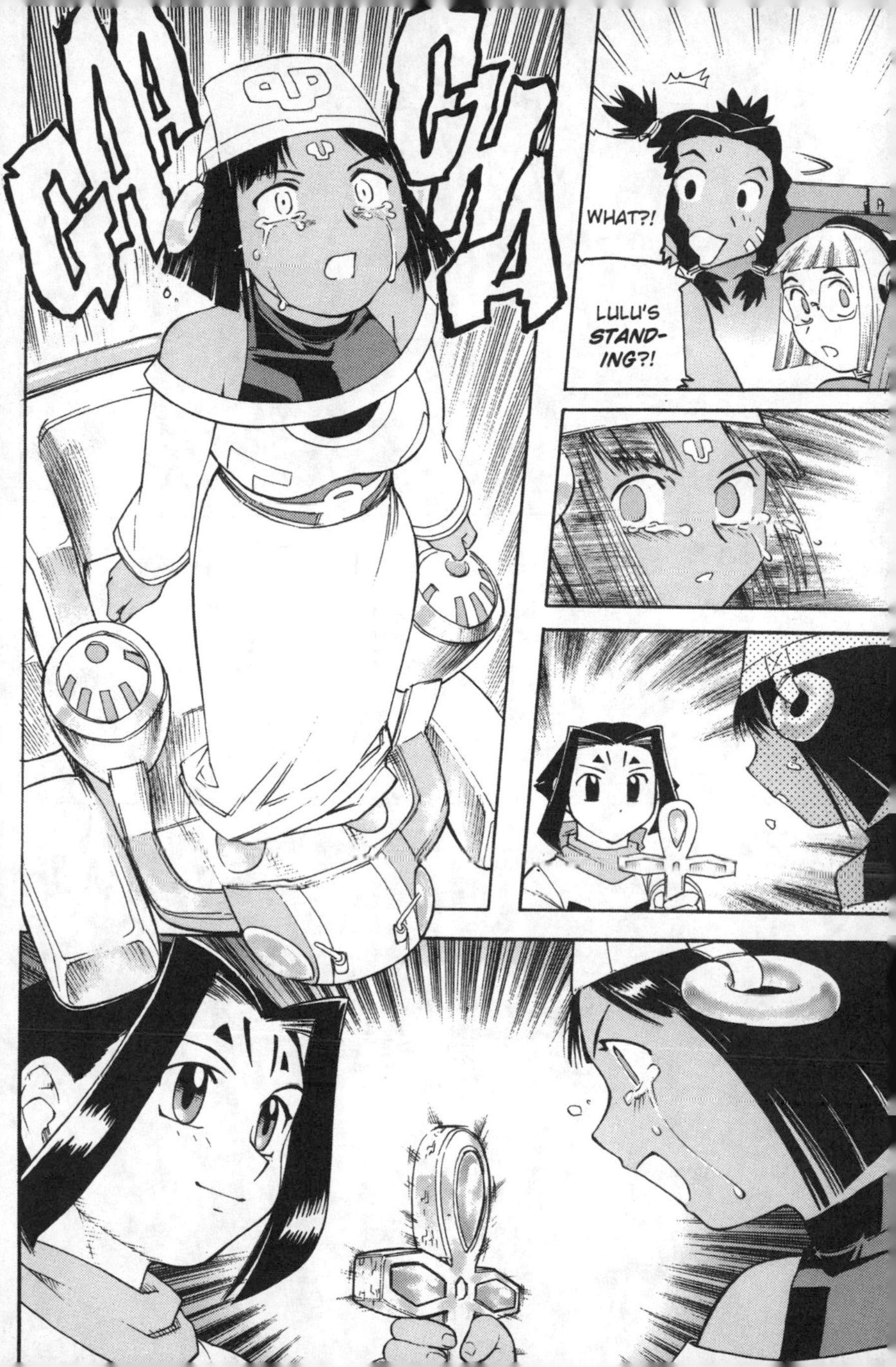

CHA CHA
WHAT?!
LULU'S STANDING?!

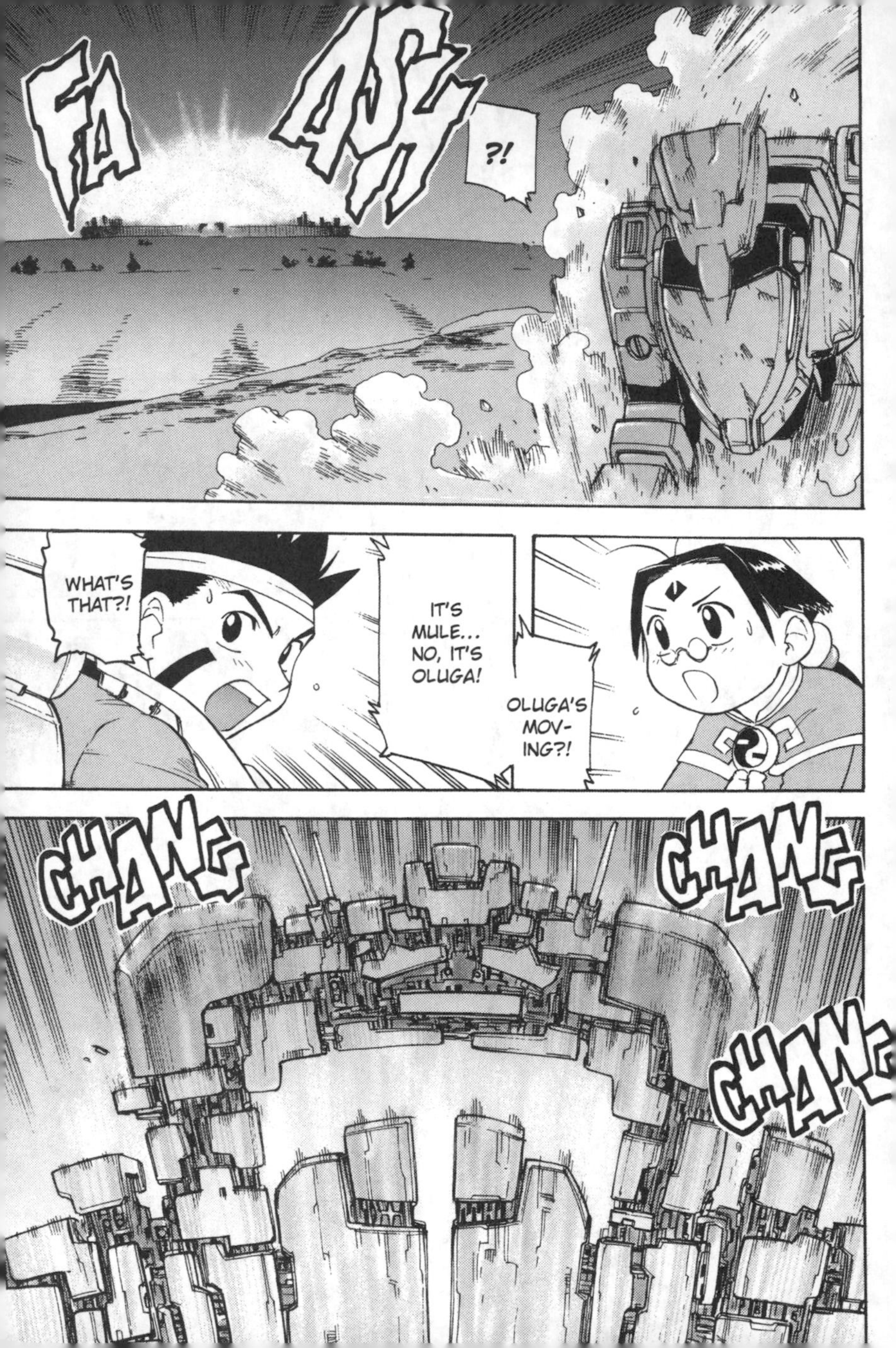
FAAASH
?!
WHAT'S THAT?!
IT'S MULE... NO, IT'S OLUGA!
OLUGA'S MOV-ING?!
CHANG
CHANG
CHANG

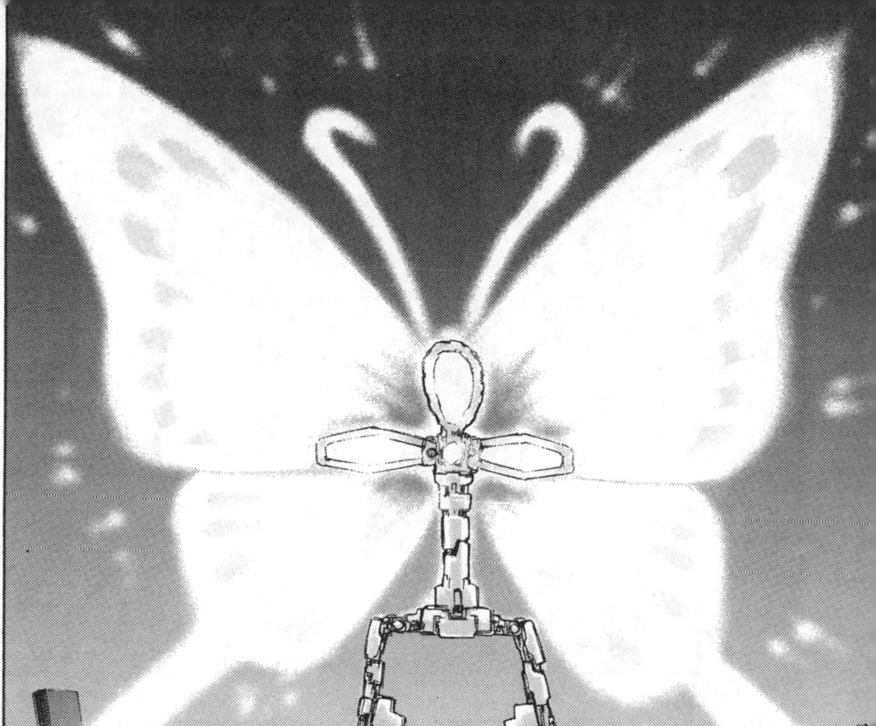
DM
DM
DM
DM
DM
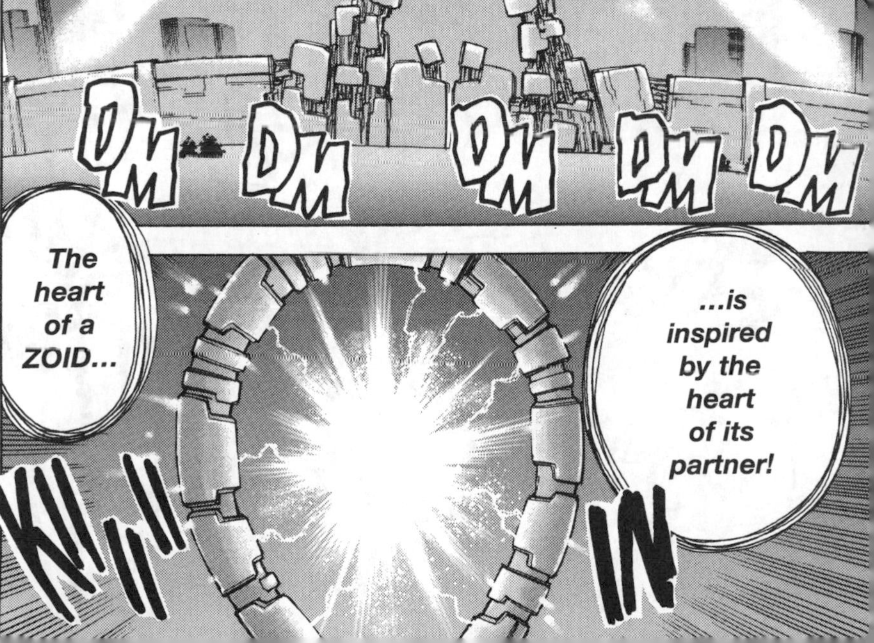
The heart of a ZOID...
KI
...is inspired by the heart of its partner!
IN

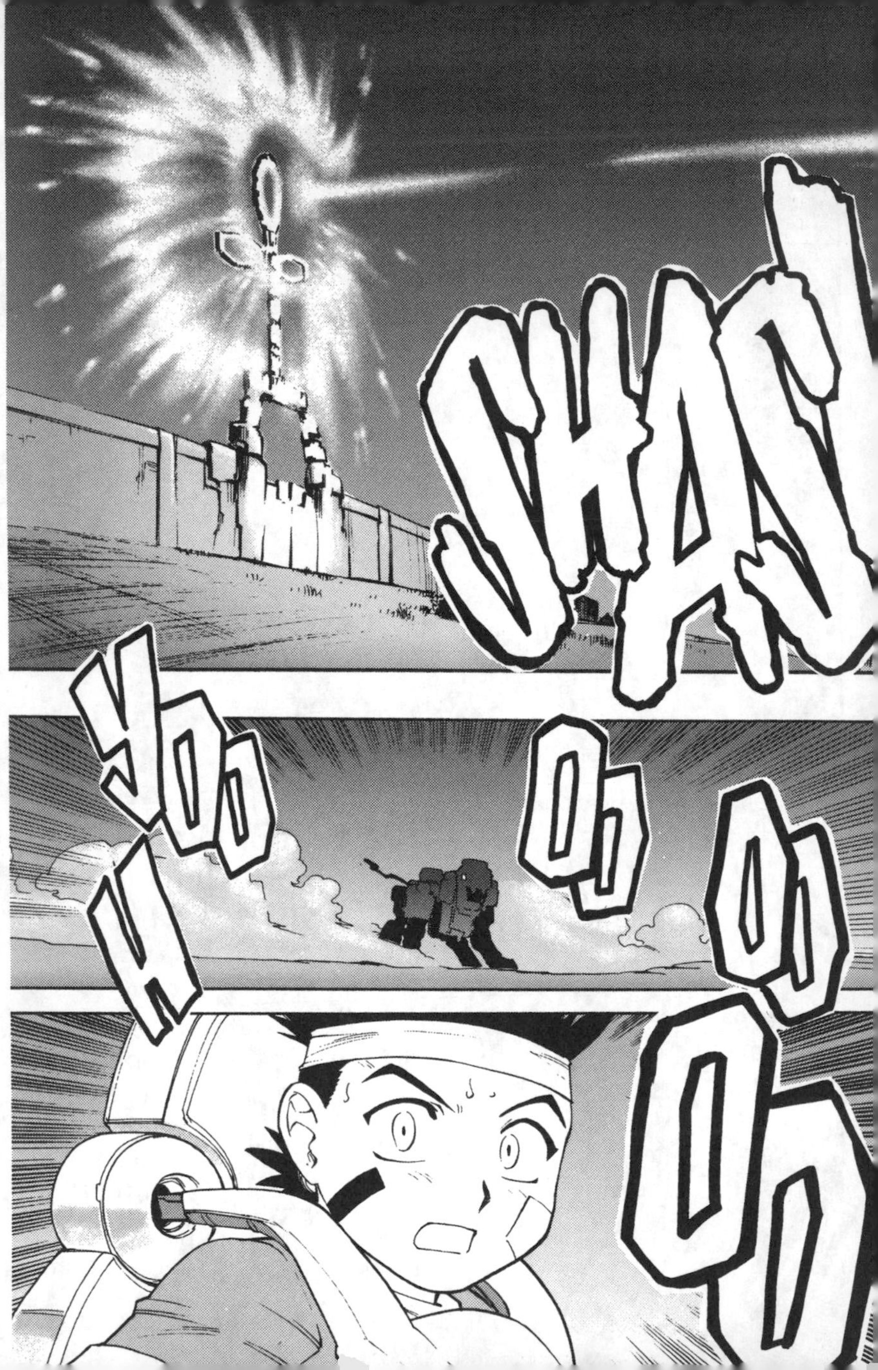
CHAN

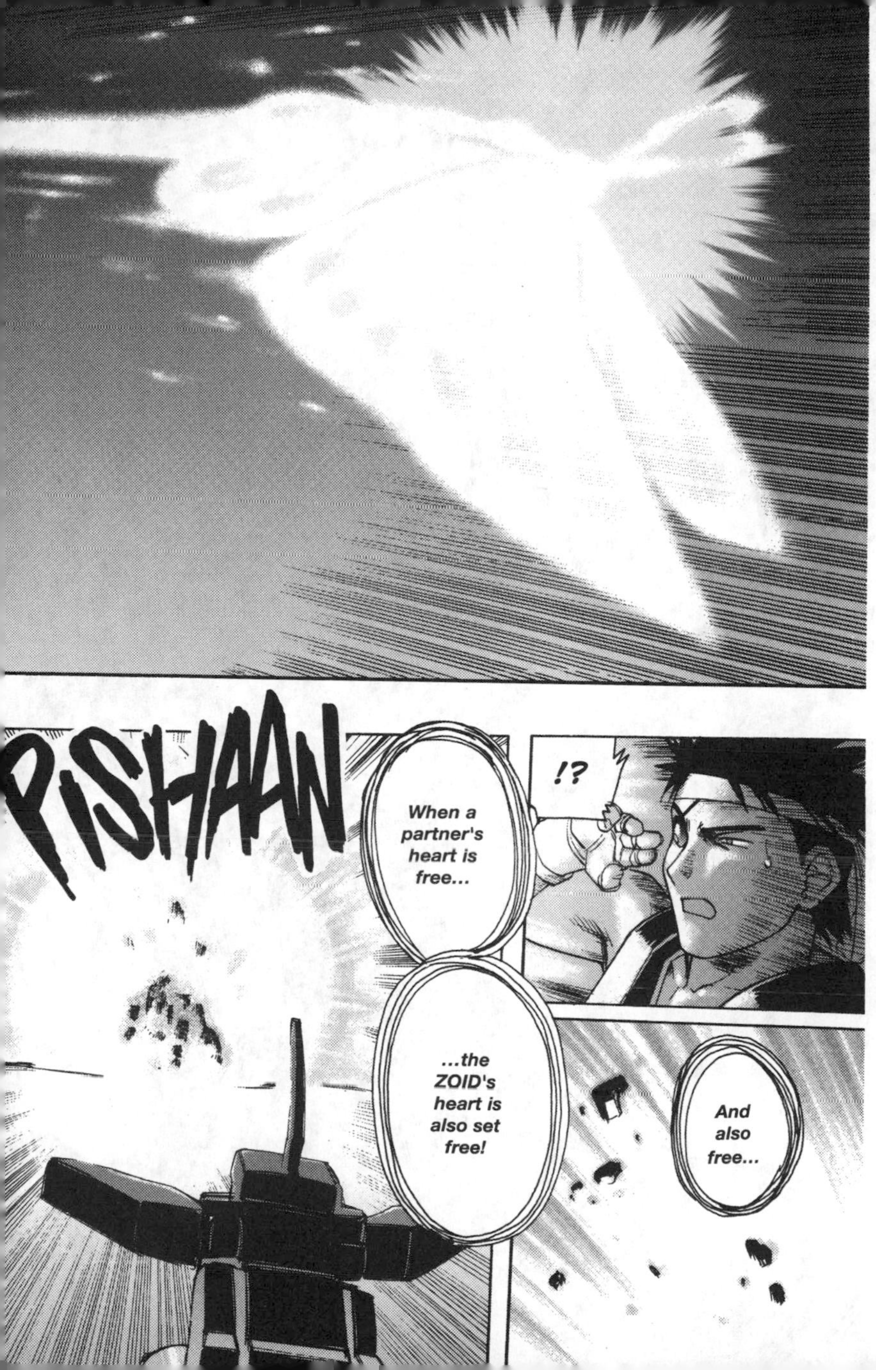
PISHAAN
When a partner's heart is free...
!?
...the ZOID's heart is also set free!
And also free...

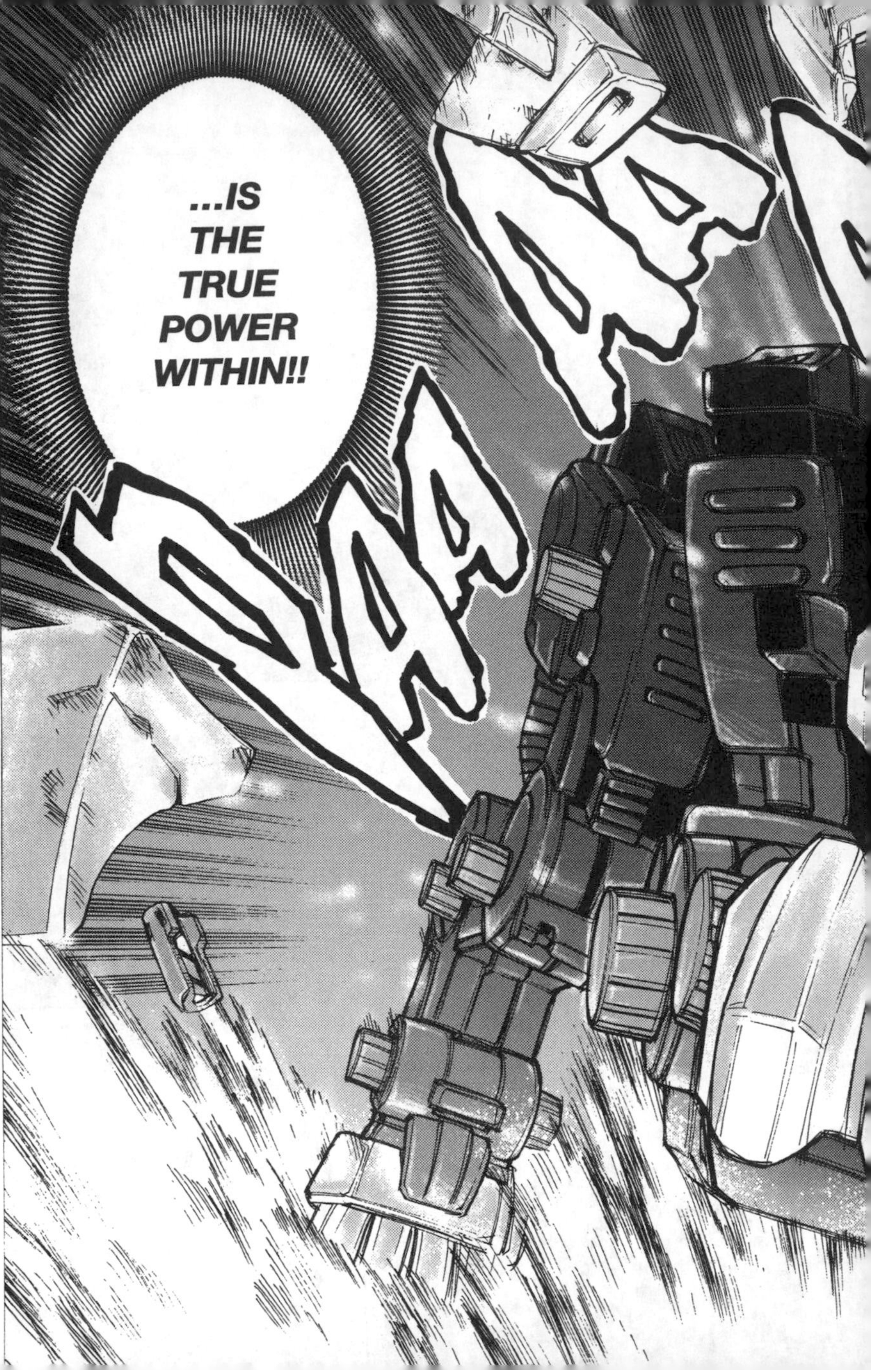
...IS THE TRUE POWER WITHIN!!

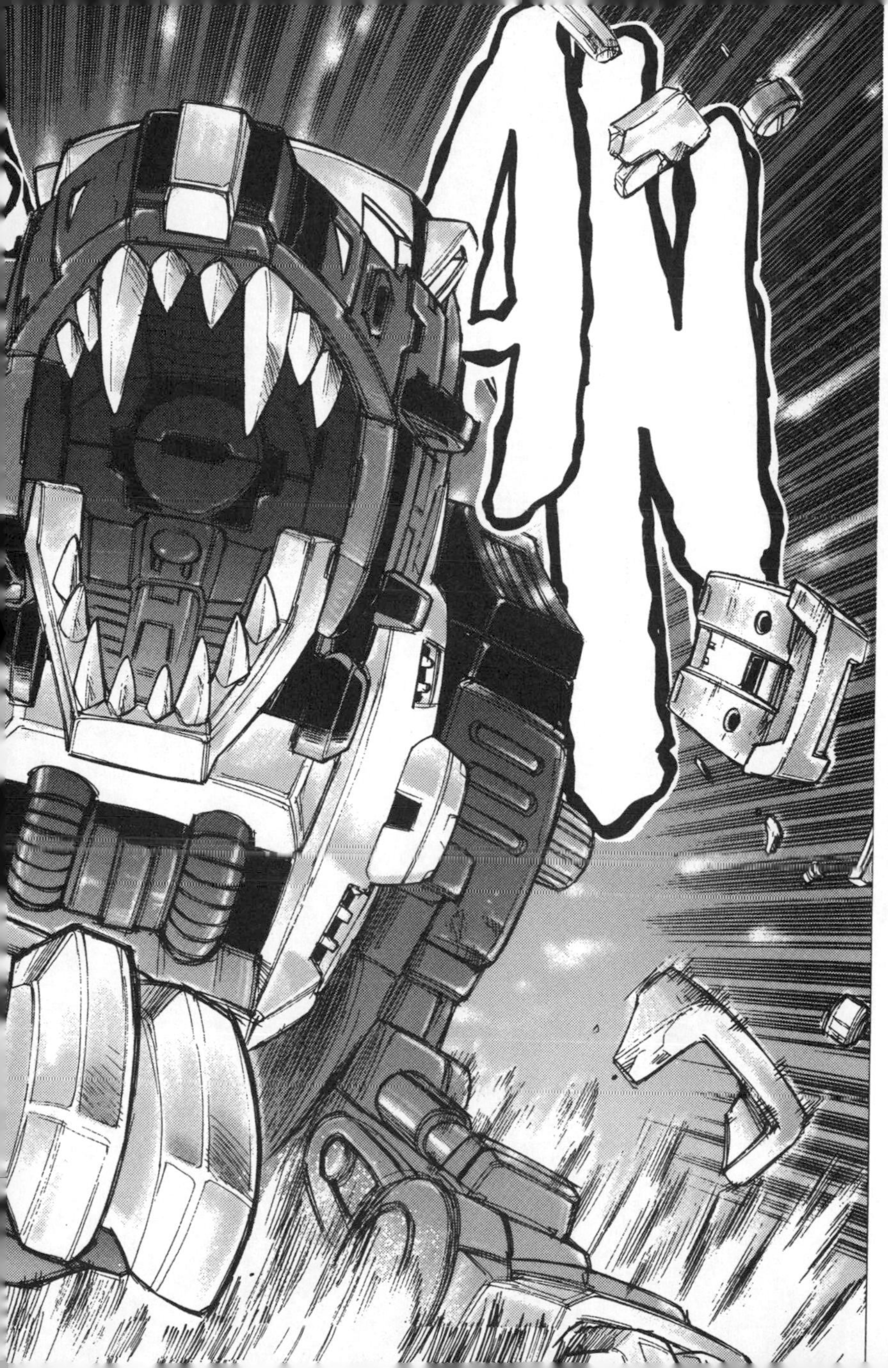

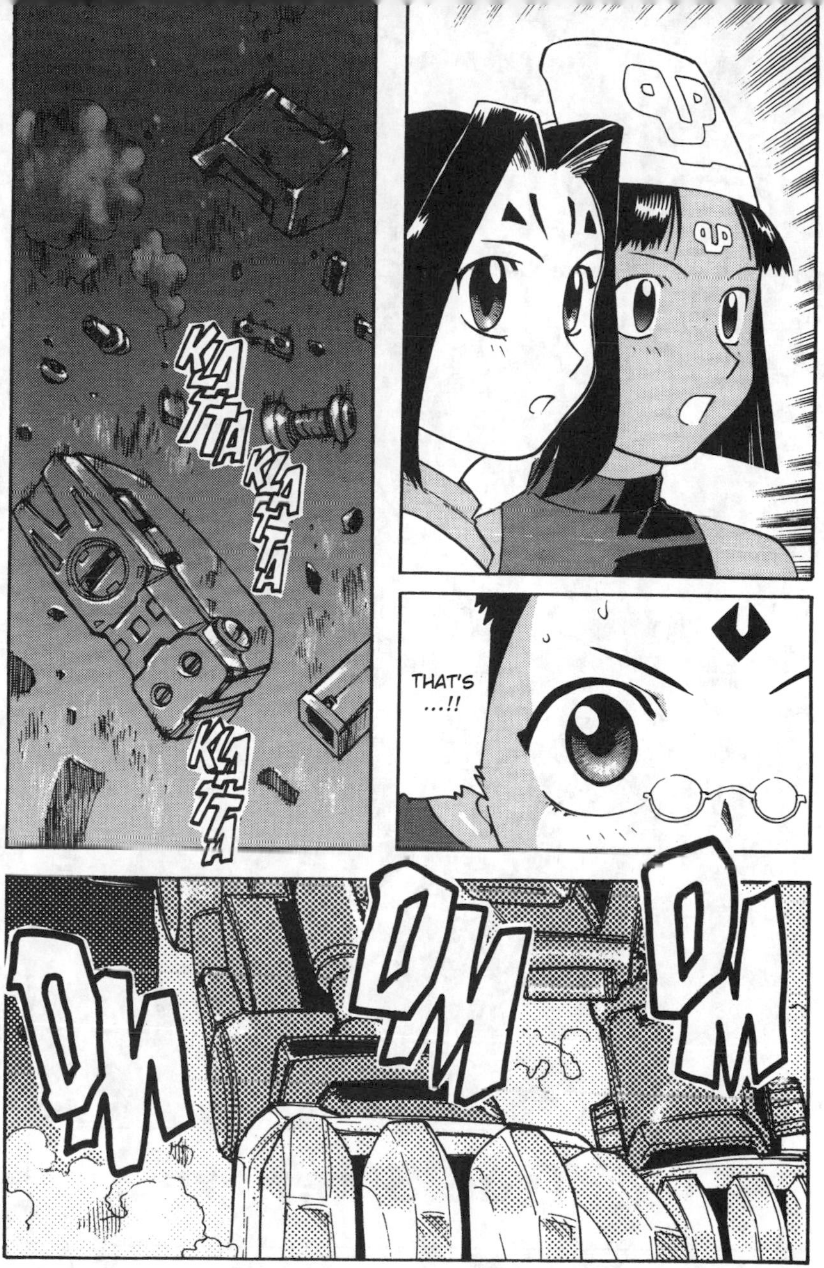
KLATTA KLATTA
KLATTA
THAT'S ...!!
DM DM DM

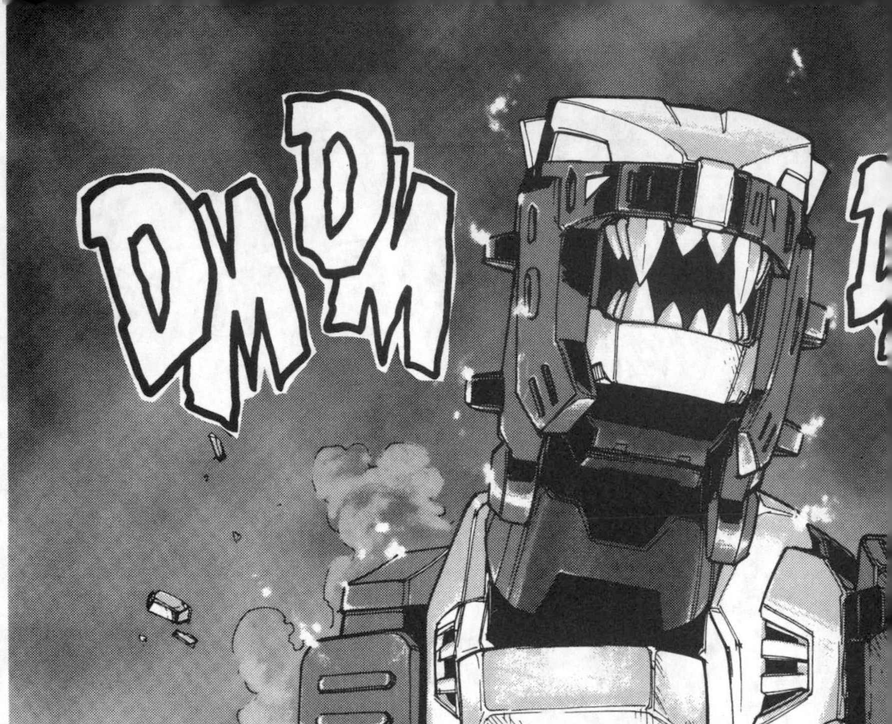
DMDM

True Strength

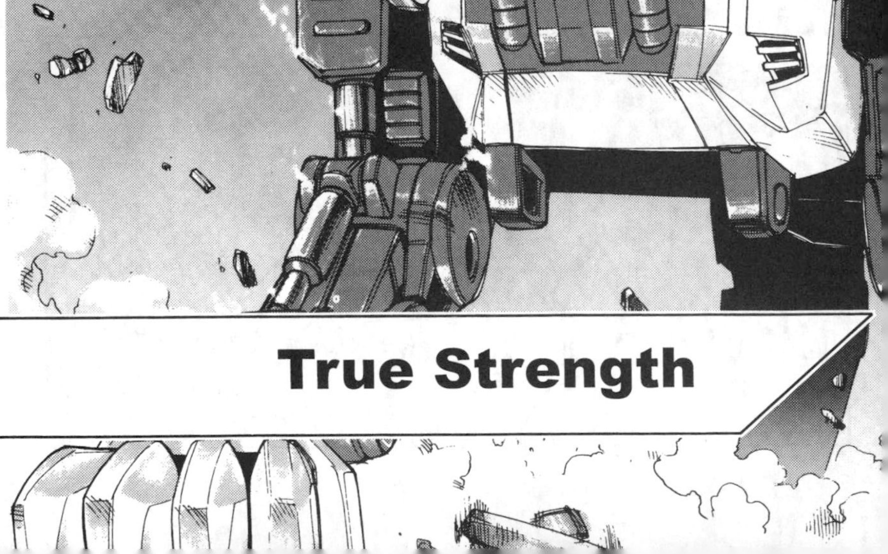

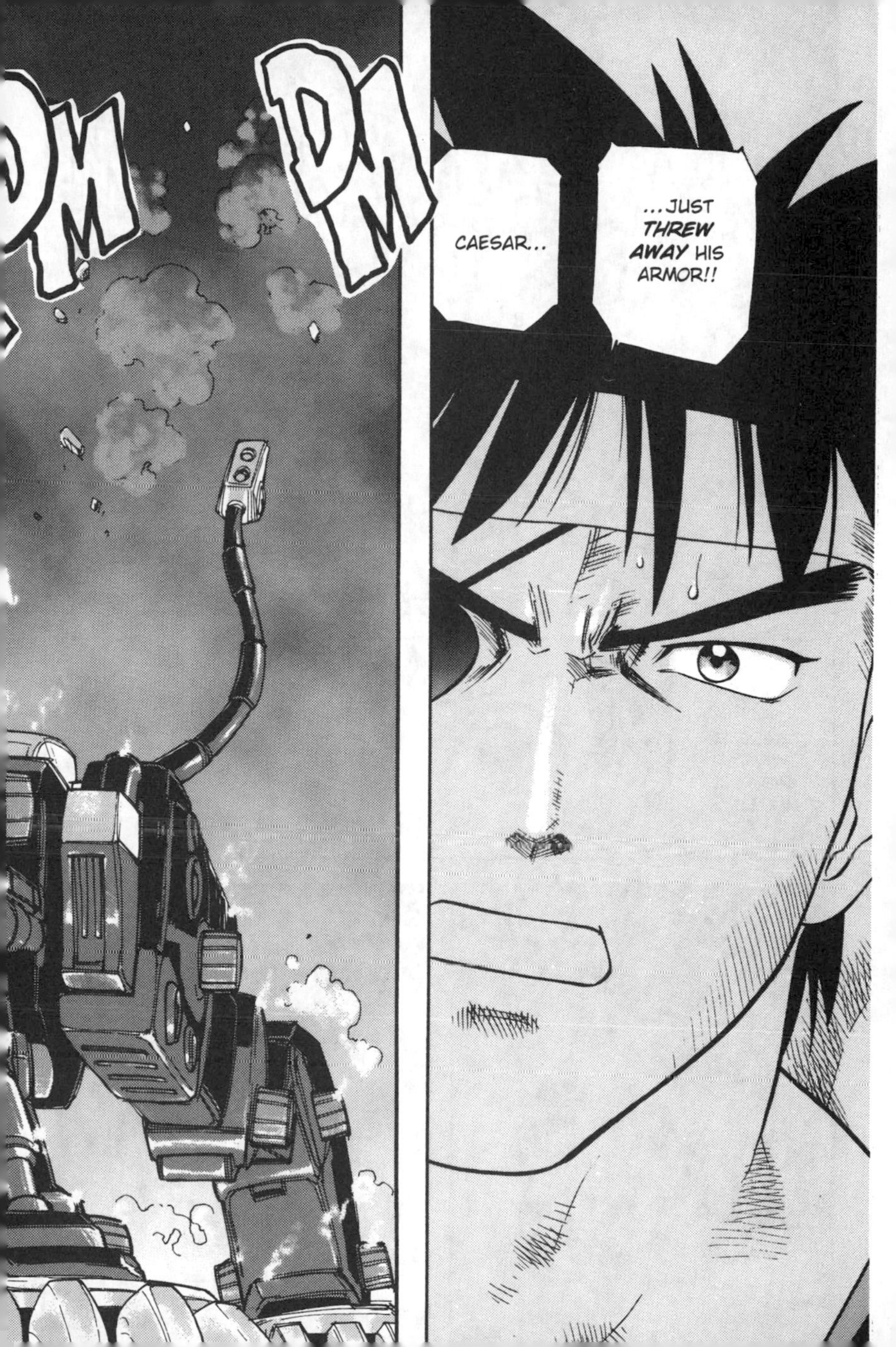
CAESAR...
...JUST **THREW AWAY** HIS ARMOR!!

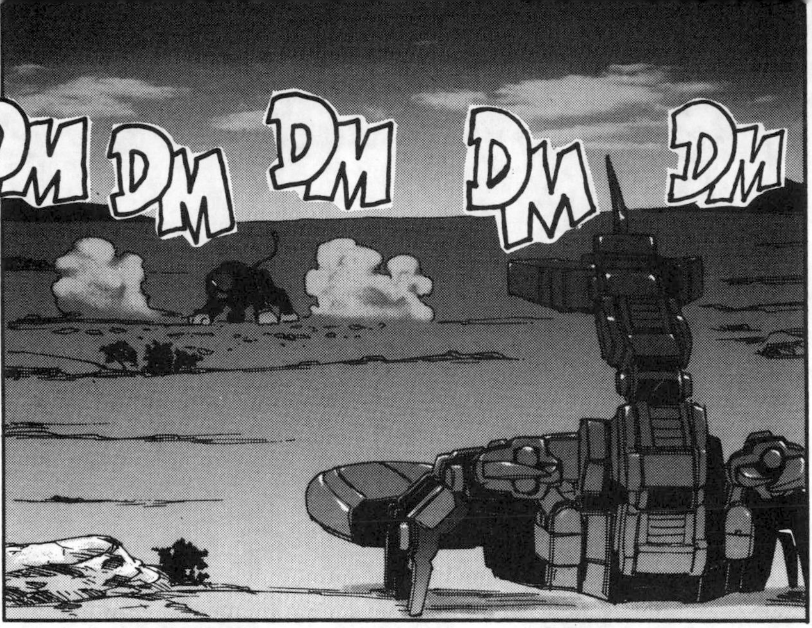
DM DM DM DM DM

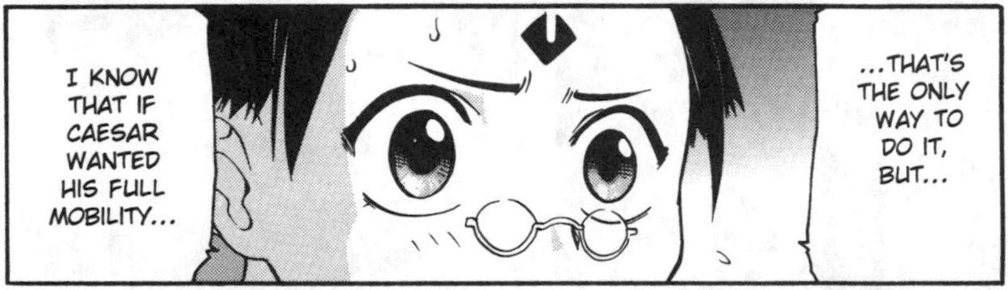
I KNOW THAT IF CAESAR WANTED HIS FULL MOBILITY...
...THAT'S THE ONLY WAY TO DO IT, BUT...

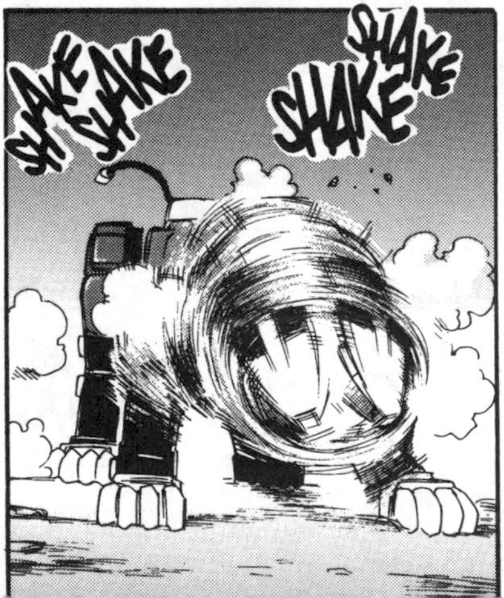
SHAKE SHAKE
SHAKE SHAKE

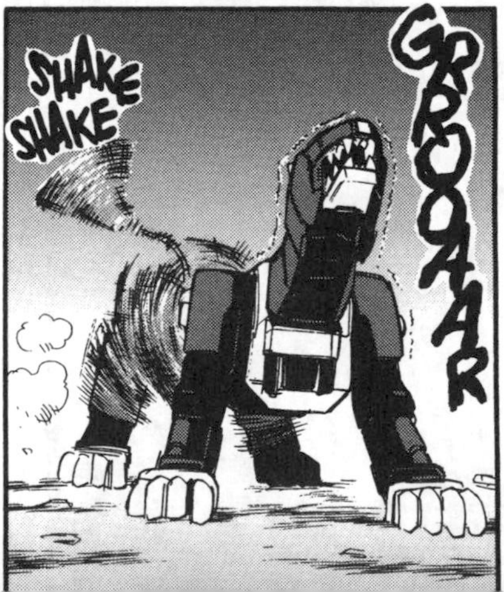
SHAKE SHAKE
GROOOAAR

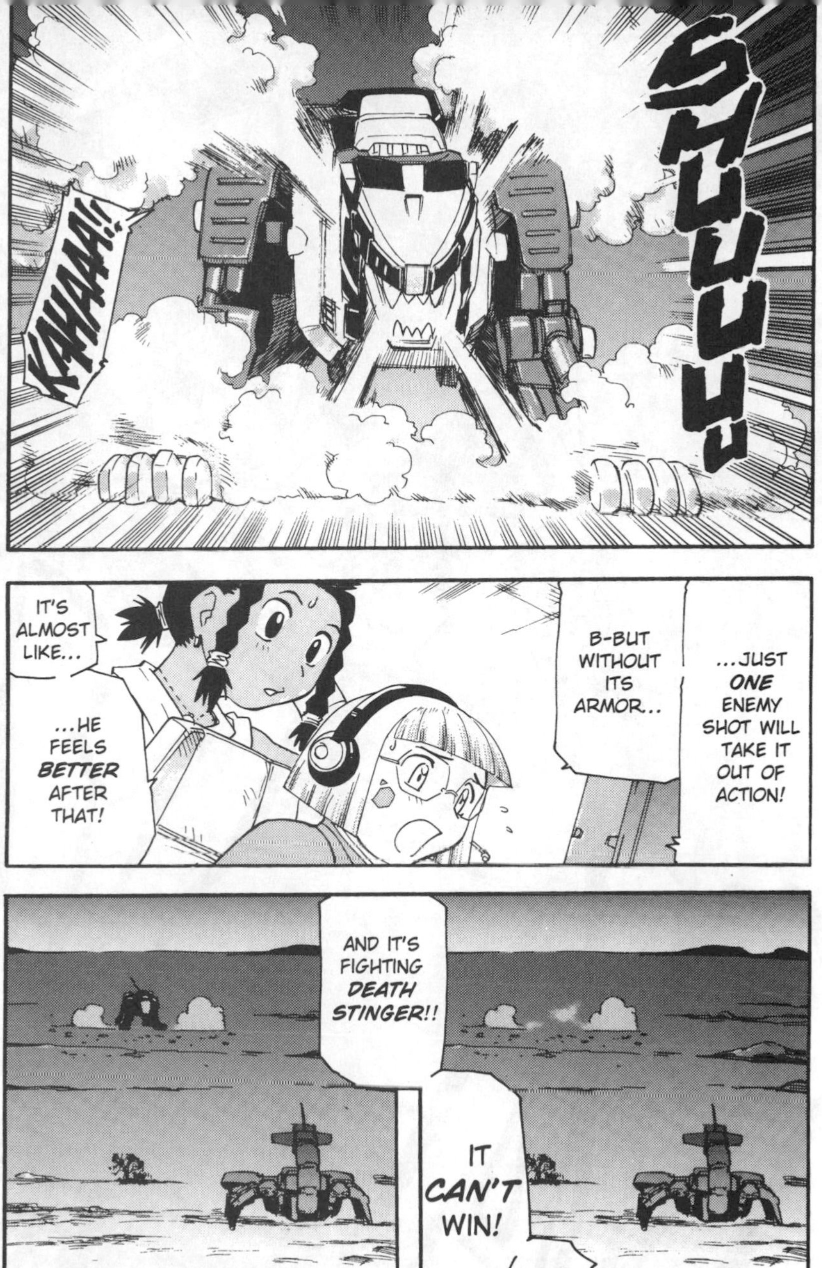
KAHAAA!!
SHULULULU
IT'S ALMOST LIKE...
...HE FEELS BETTER AFTER THAT!
B-BUT WITHOUT ITS ARMOR...
...JUST ONE ENEMY SHOT WILL TAKE IT OUT OF ACTION!
AND IT'S FIGHTING DEATH STINGER!!
IT CAN'T WIN!
?!

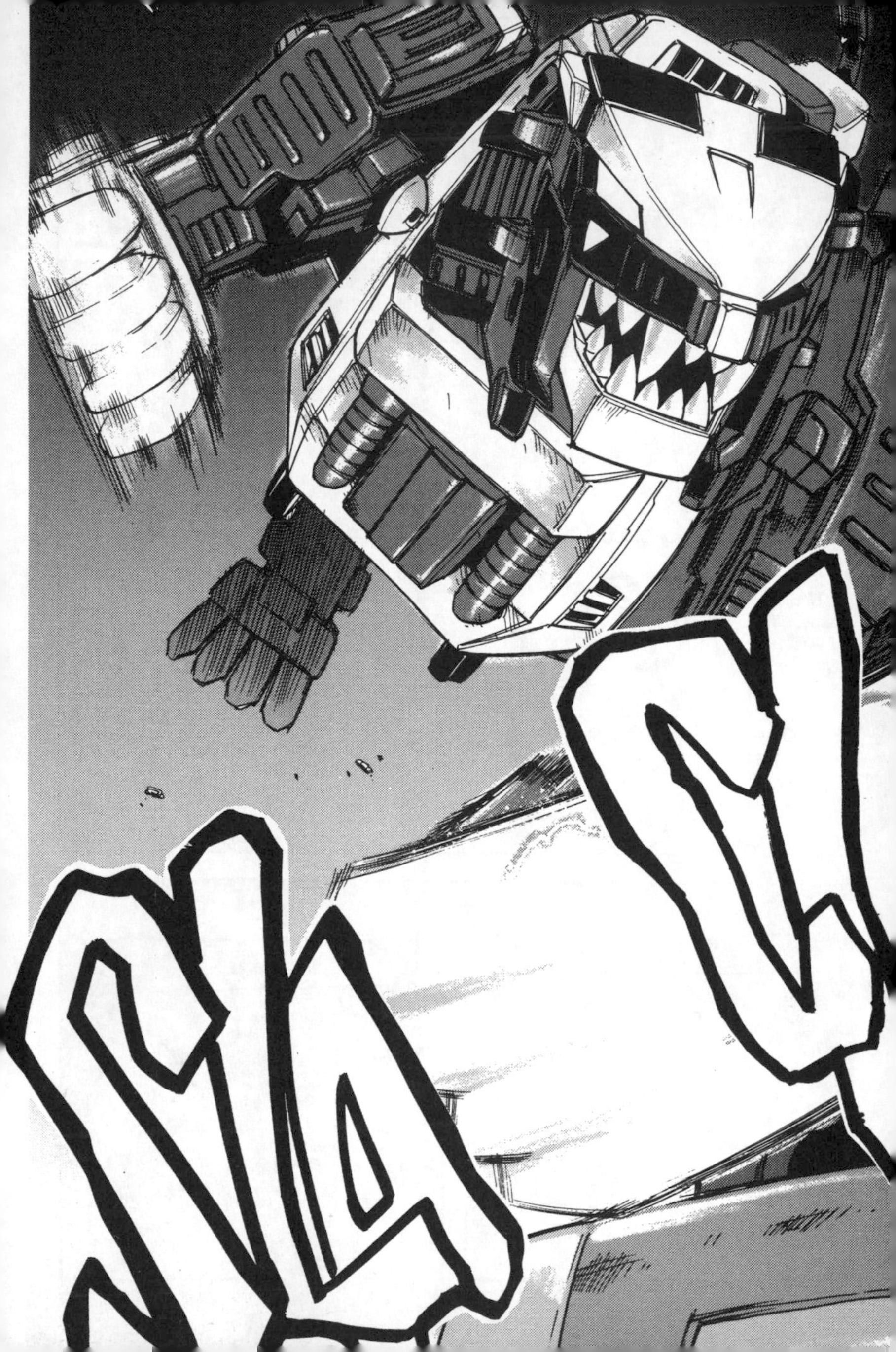

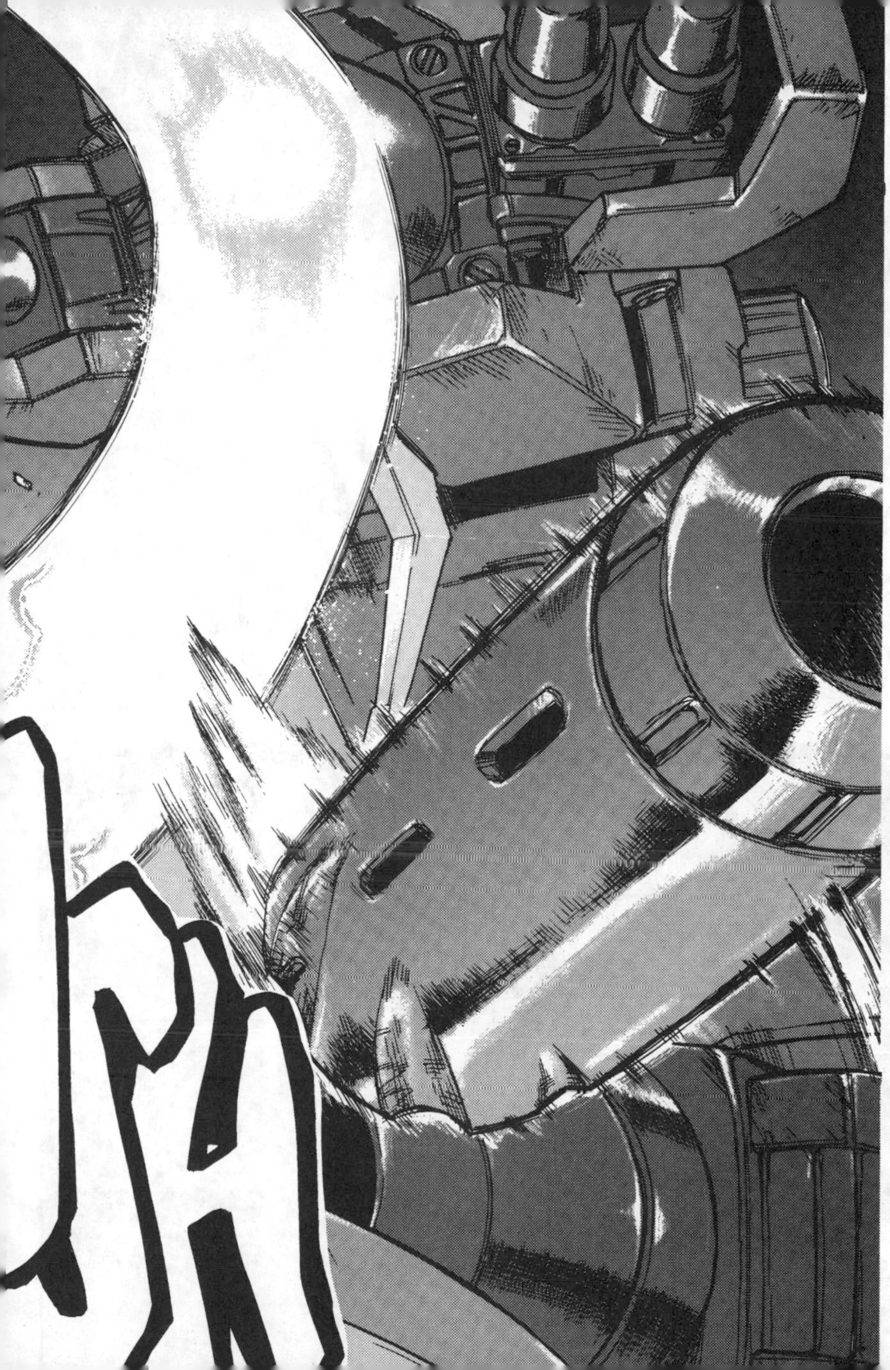

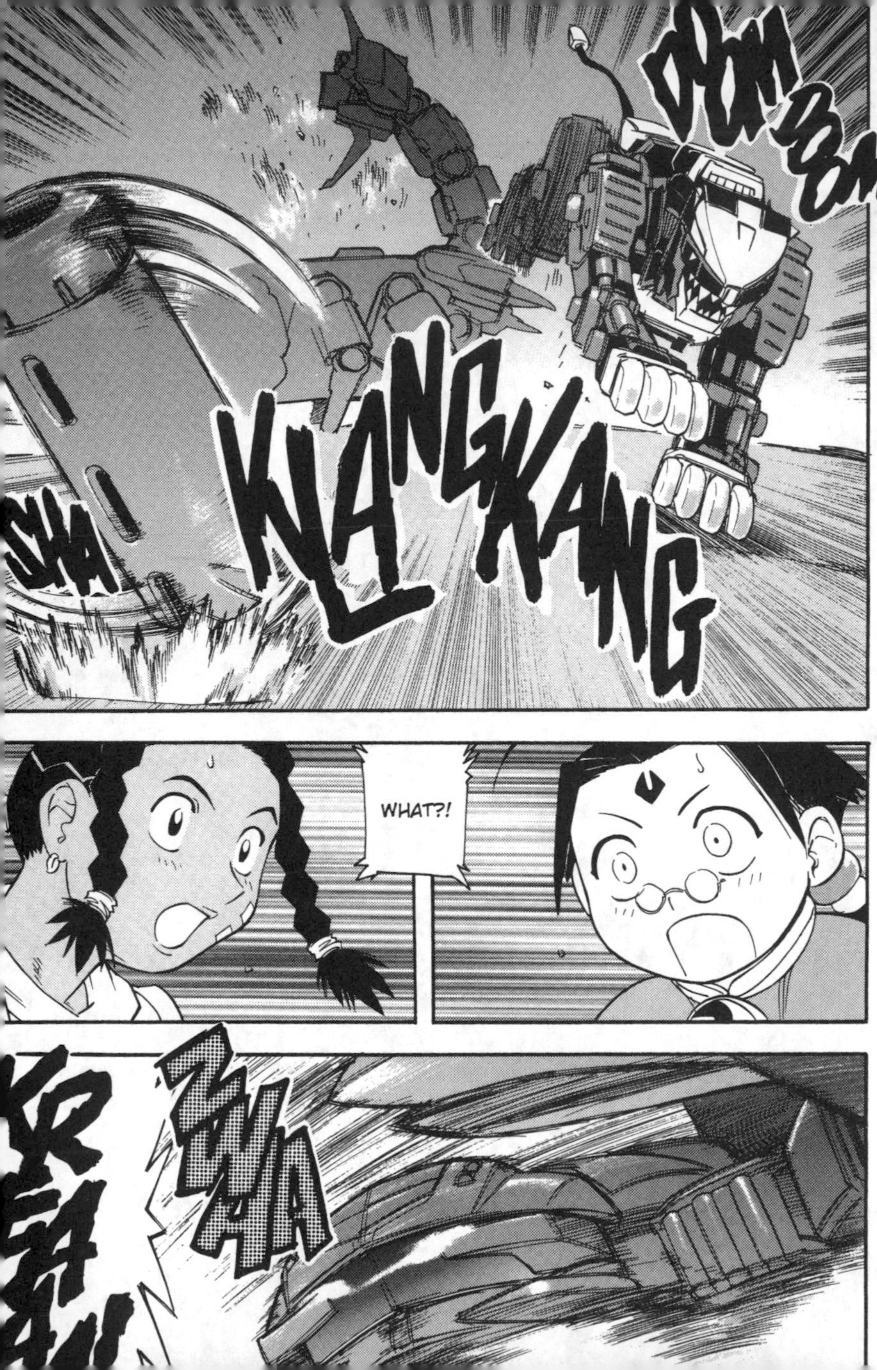
DOOM BOOM
SHA
KLANGKANG
WHAT?!
ZWHA

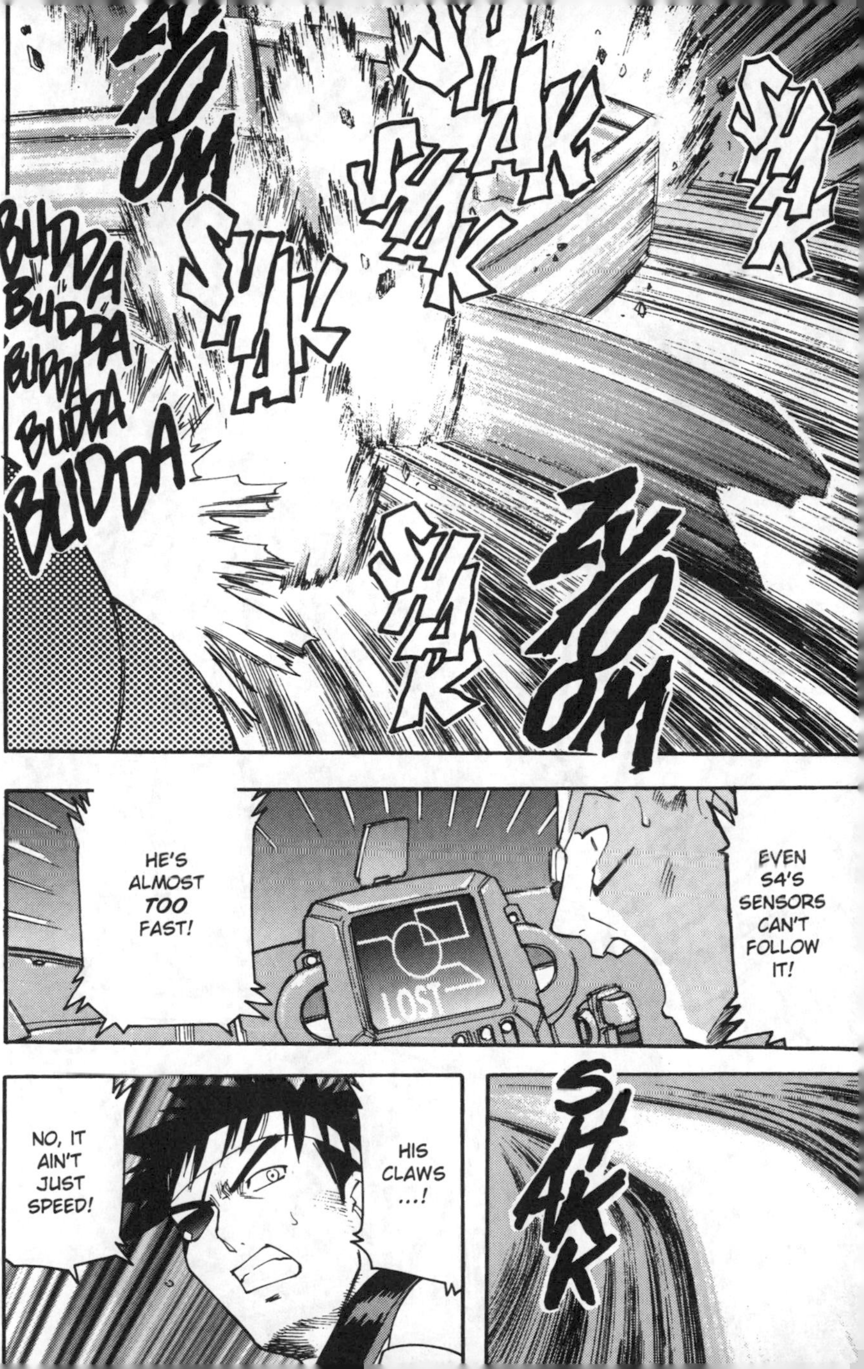
ZYOOM
SHAK
SHAK
SHAK
BUDDA BUDDA BUDDA BUDDA BUDDA
SHAK
SHAK
ZYOOM
HE'S ALMOST *TOO* FAST!
LOST
EVEN S4'S SENSORS CAN'T FOLLOW IT!
NO, IT AIN'T JUST SPEED!
HIS CLAWS ...!
SHAK

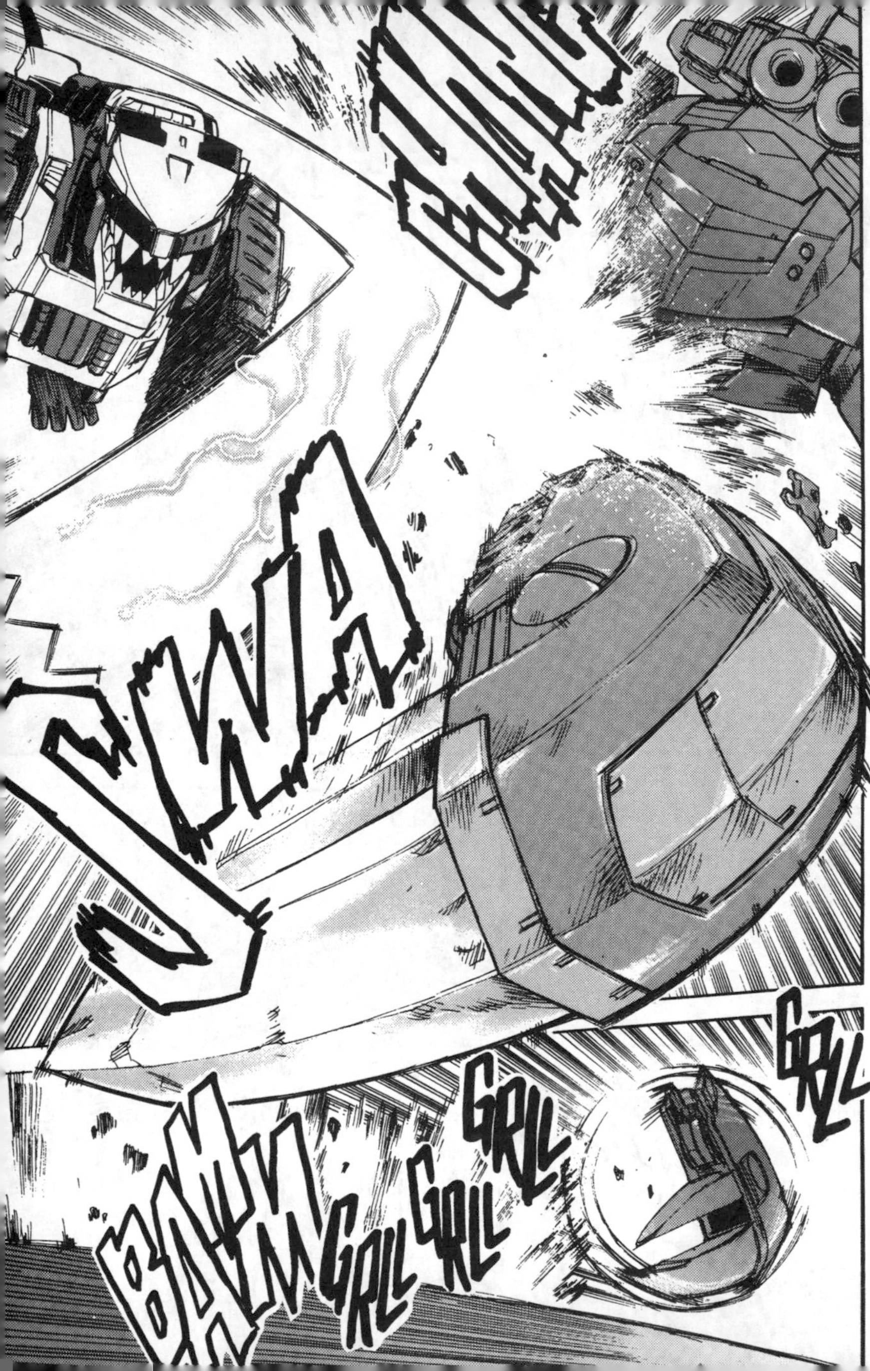
GRLL
GRLL
GRLL
GRLL

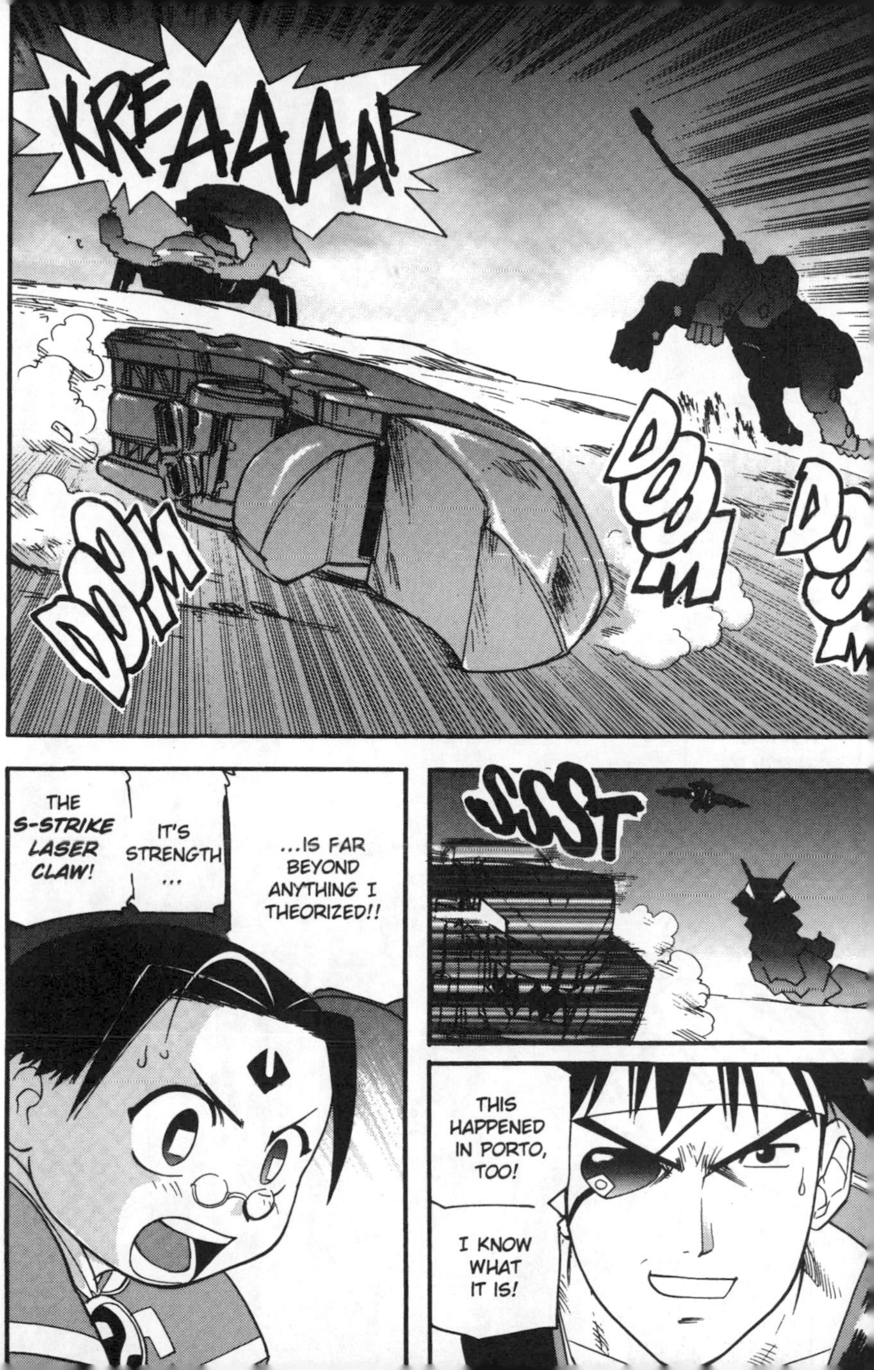
KREAAAA!
DOOM
DOOM
DOOM
THE S-STRIKE LASER CLAW!
IT'S STRENGTH...
...IS FAR BEYOND ANYTHING I THEORIZED!!
SSST
THIS HAPPENED IN PORTO, TOO!
I KNOW WHAT IT IS!

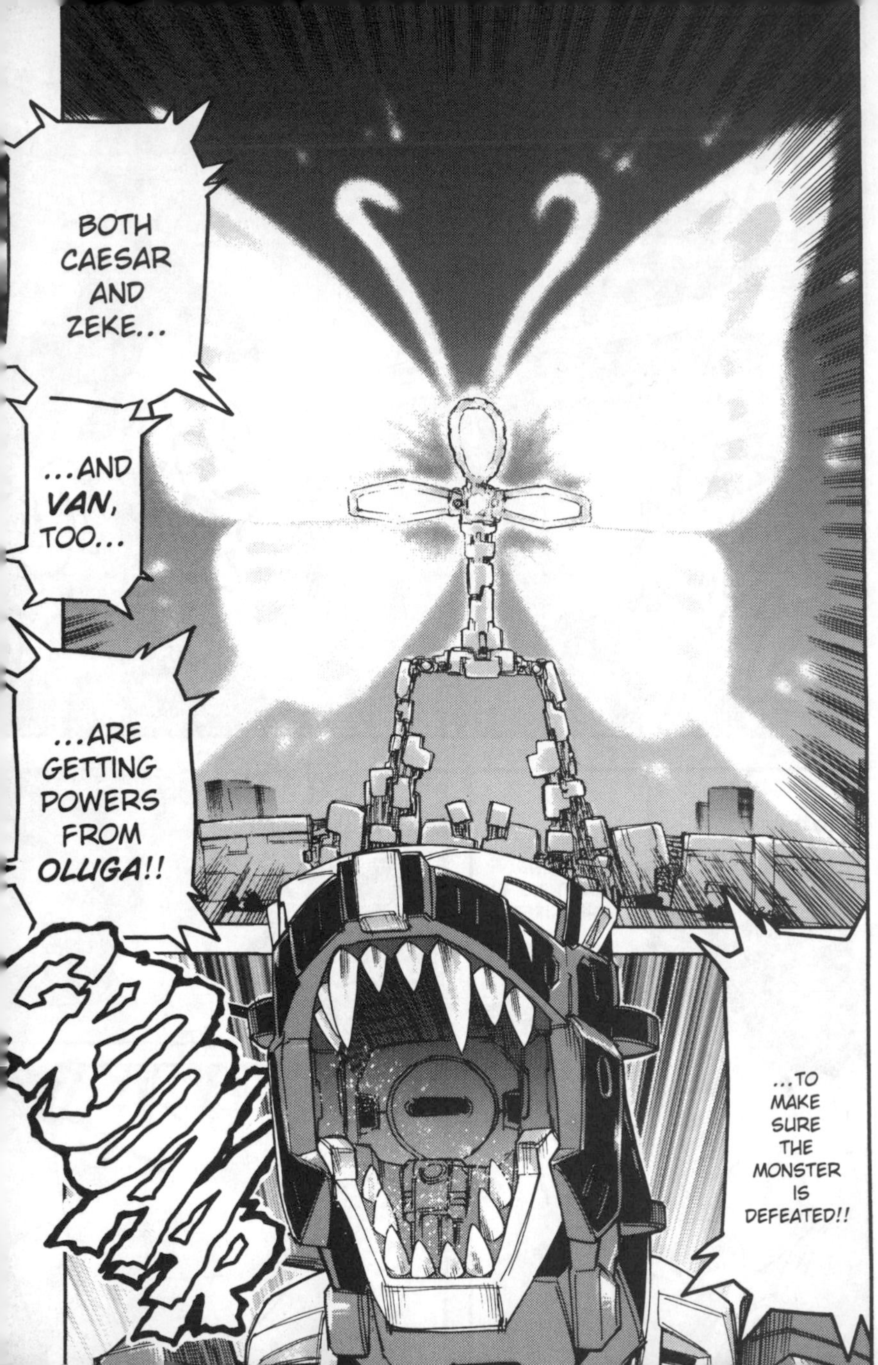
BOTH CAESAR AND ZEKE...
...AND VAN, TOO...
...ARE GETTING POWERS FROM OLUGA!!
...TO MAKE SURE THE MONSTER IS DEFEATED!!

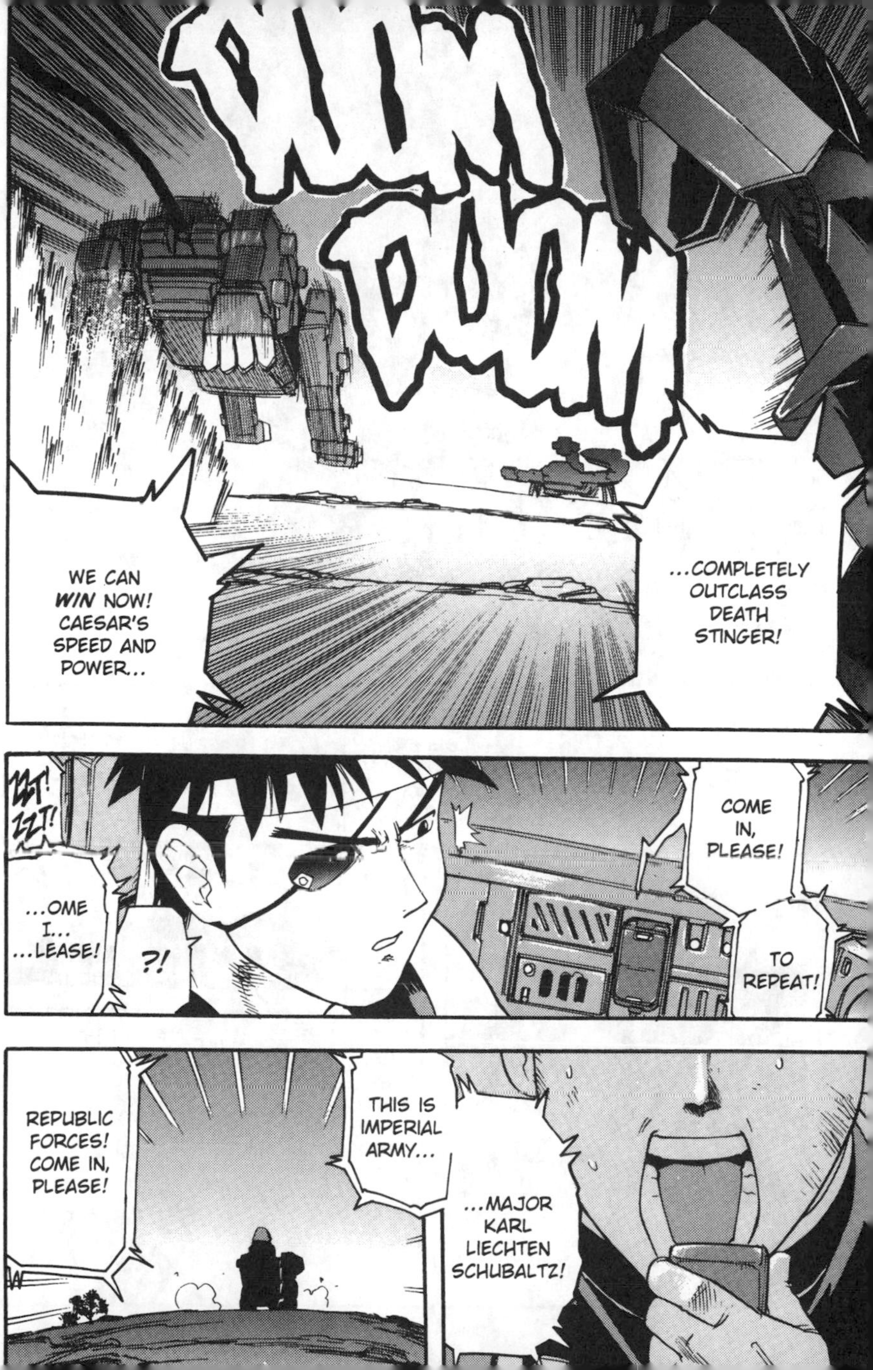
DUM
DUM
WE CAN *WIN* NOW! CAESAR'S SPEED AND POWER...
...COMPLETELY OUTCLASS DEATH STINGER!
ZZT! ZZT!
...OME I... ...LEASE!
?!
COME IN, PLEASE!
TO REPEAT!
REPUBLIC FORCES! COME IN, PLEASE!
THIS IS IMPERIAL ARMY...
...MAJOR KARL LIECHTEN SCHUBALTZ!

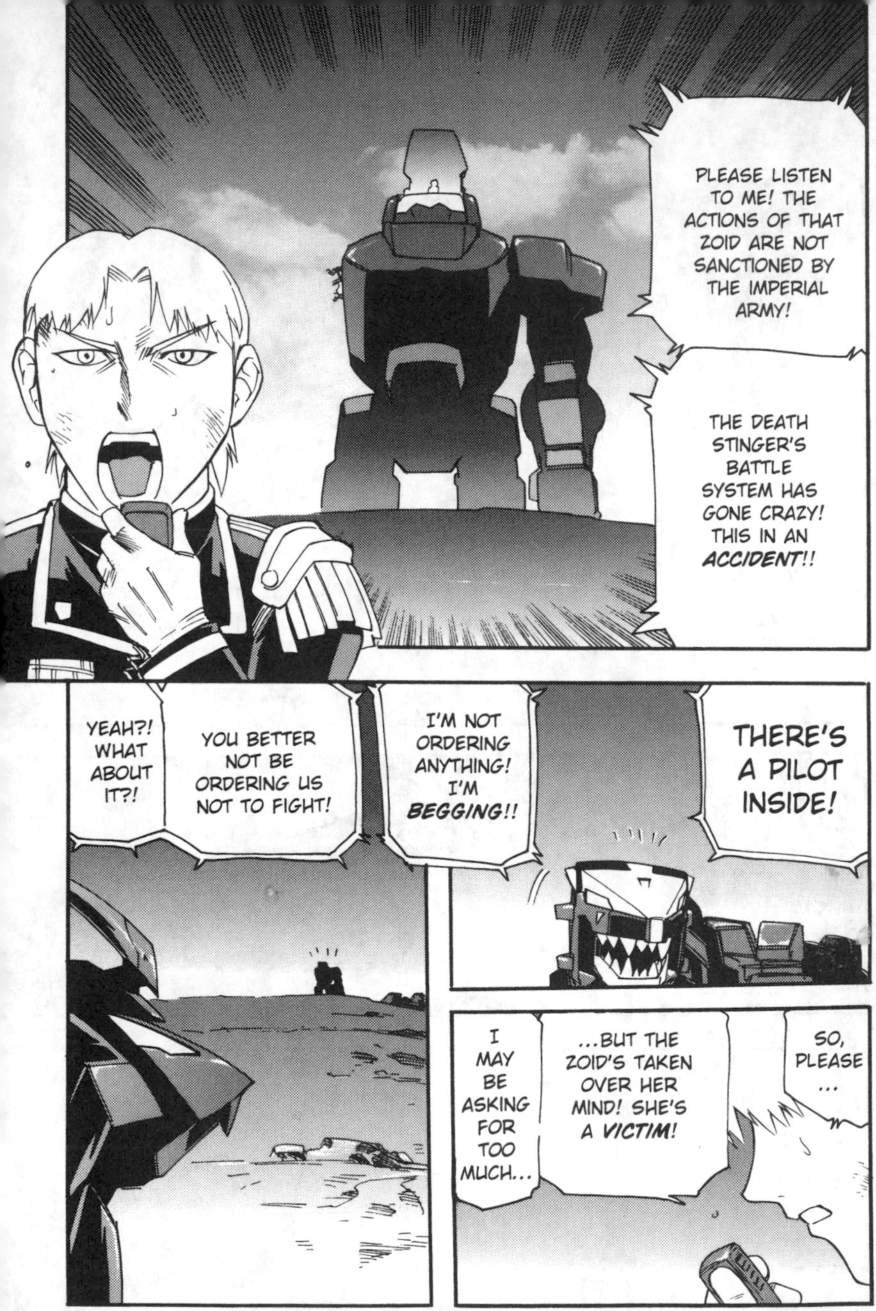

PLEASE LISTEN TO ME! THE ACTIONS OF THAT ZOID ARE NOT SANCTIONED BY THE IMPERIAL ARMY!
THE DEATH STINGER'S BATTLE SYSTEM HAS GONE CRAZY! THIS IN AN *ACCIDENT*!!
YEAH?! WHAT ABOUT IT?!
YOU BETTER NOT BE ORDERING US NOT TO FIGHT!
I'M NOT ORDERING ANYTHING! I'M *BEGGING*!!
THERE'S A PILOT INSIDE!
I MAY BE ASKING FOR TOO MUCH...
...BUT THE ZOID'S TAKEN OVER HER MIND! SHE'S A *VICTIM*!
SO, PLEASE ...

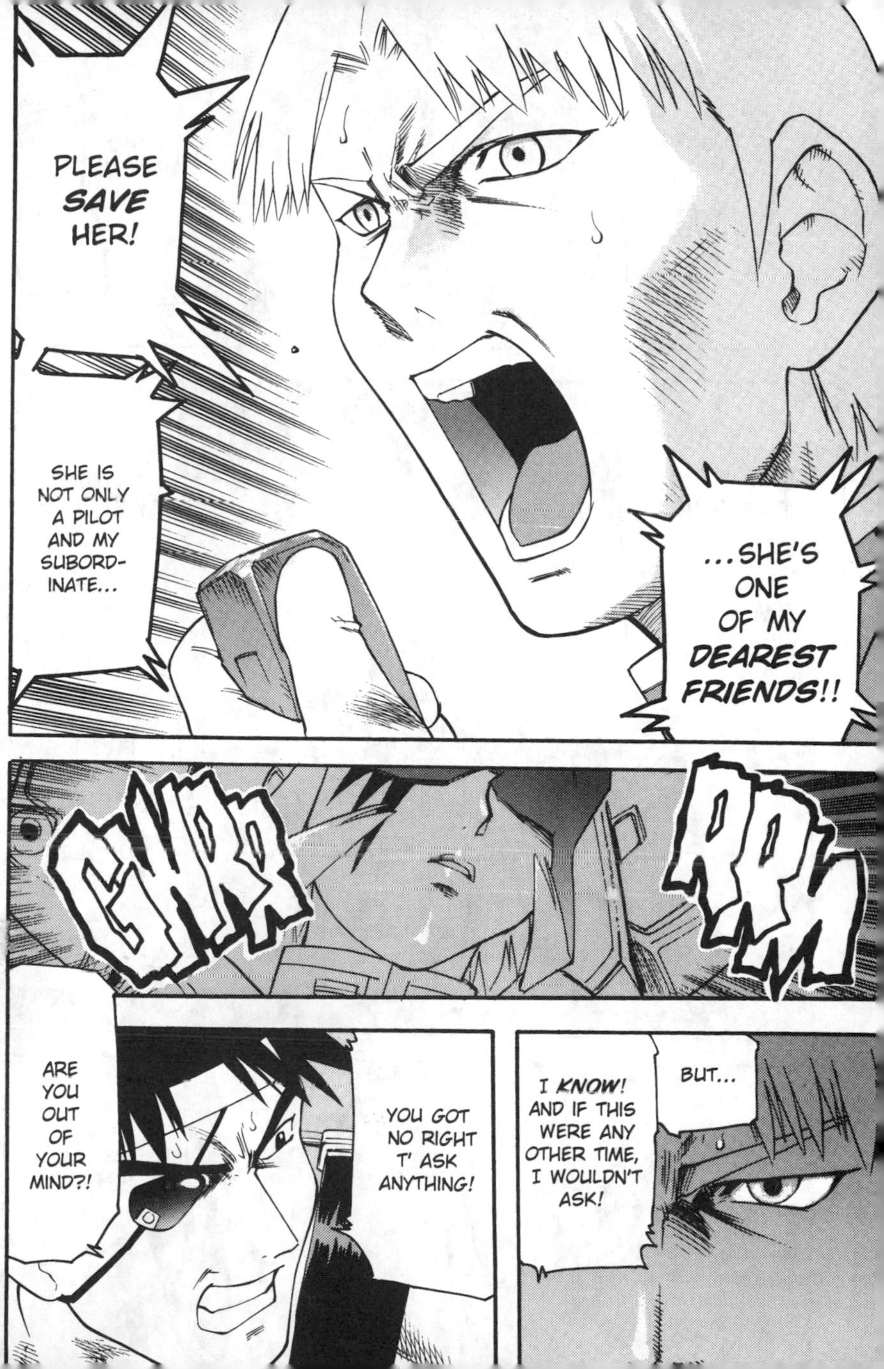

PLEASE SAVE HER!
SHE IS NOT ONLY A PILOT AND MY SUBORD-INATE...
...SHE'S ONE OF MY DEAREST FRIENDS!!
CHRRRRM
ARE YOU OUT OF YOUR MIND?!
YOU GOT NO RIGHT T' ASK ANYTHING!
I KNOW! AND IF THIS WERE ANY OTHER TIME, I WOULDN'T ASK!
BUT...

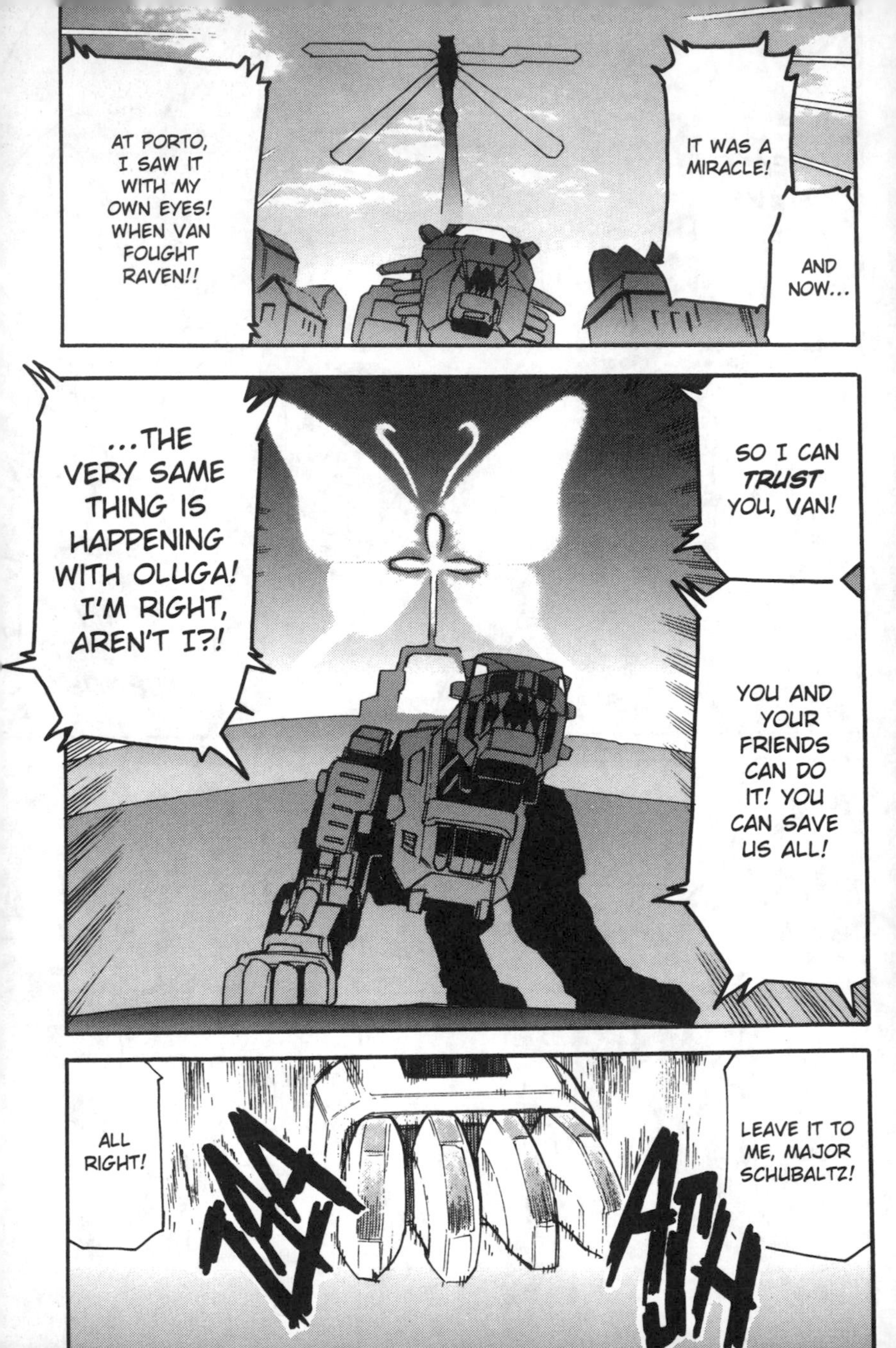
AT PORTO, I SAW IT WITH MY OWN EYES! WHEN VAN FOUGHT RAVEN!!
IT WAS A MIRACLE!
AND NOW...
...THE VERY SAME THING IS HAPPENING WITH OLUGA! I'M RIGHT, AREN'T I?!
SO I CAN *TRUST* YOU, VAN!
YOU AND YOUR FRIENDS CAN DO IT! YOU CAN SAVE US ALL!
ALL RIGHT!
LEAVE IT TO ME, MAJOR SCHUBALTZ!
ZAAAAACH

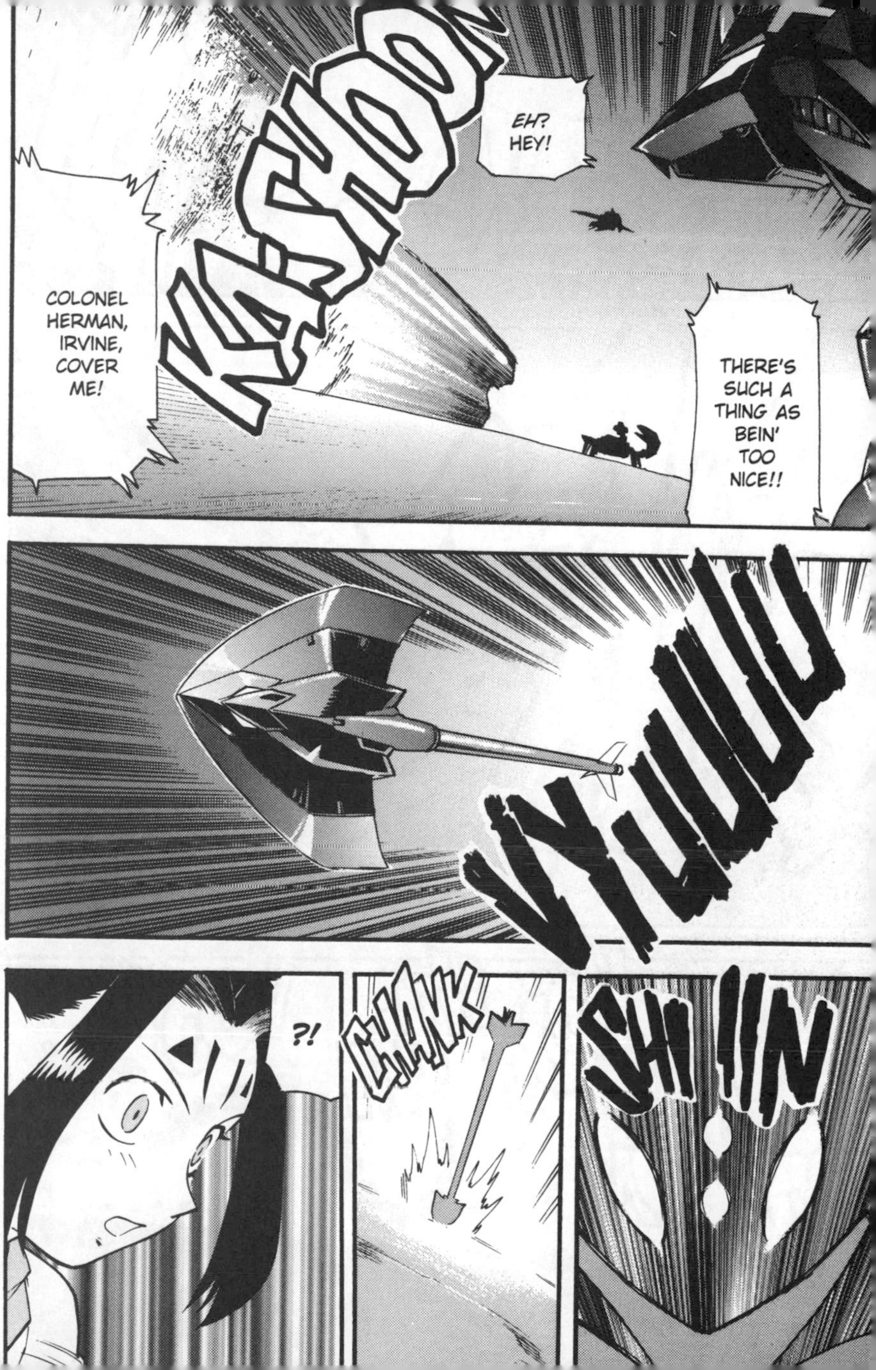
COLONEL HERMAN, IRVINE, COVER ME!
KA-CHOOM
EH? HEY!
THERE'S SUCH A THING AS BEIN' TOO NICE!!
VYUUUU
?!
CHANK
SHI IIN

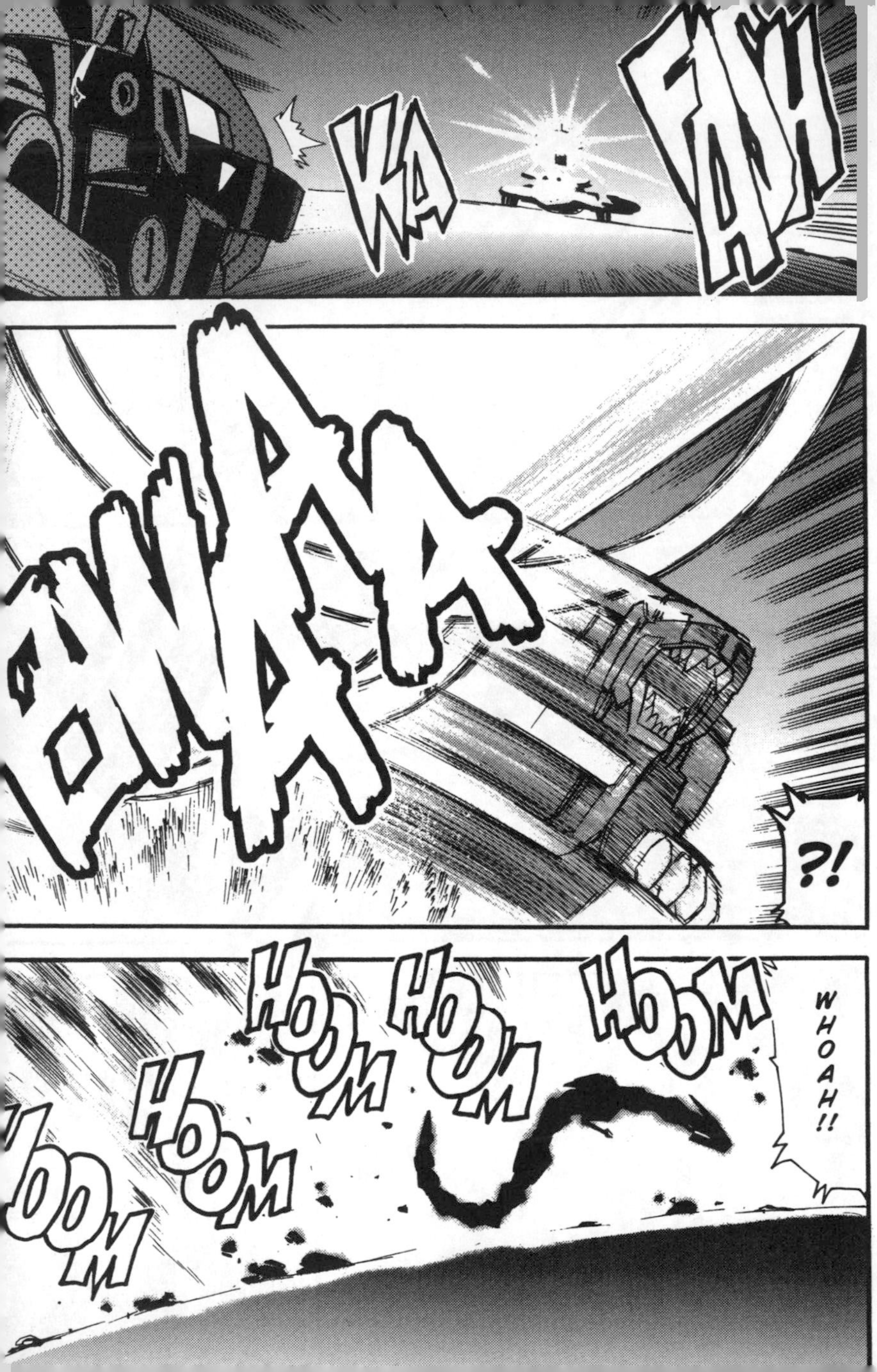
KA
FAAH
BWAAA
?!
HOOM
HOOM
HOOM
HOOM
HOOM
WHOAH!!

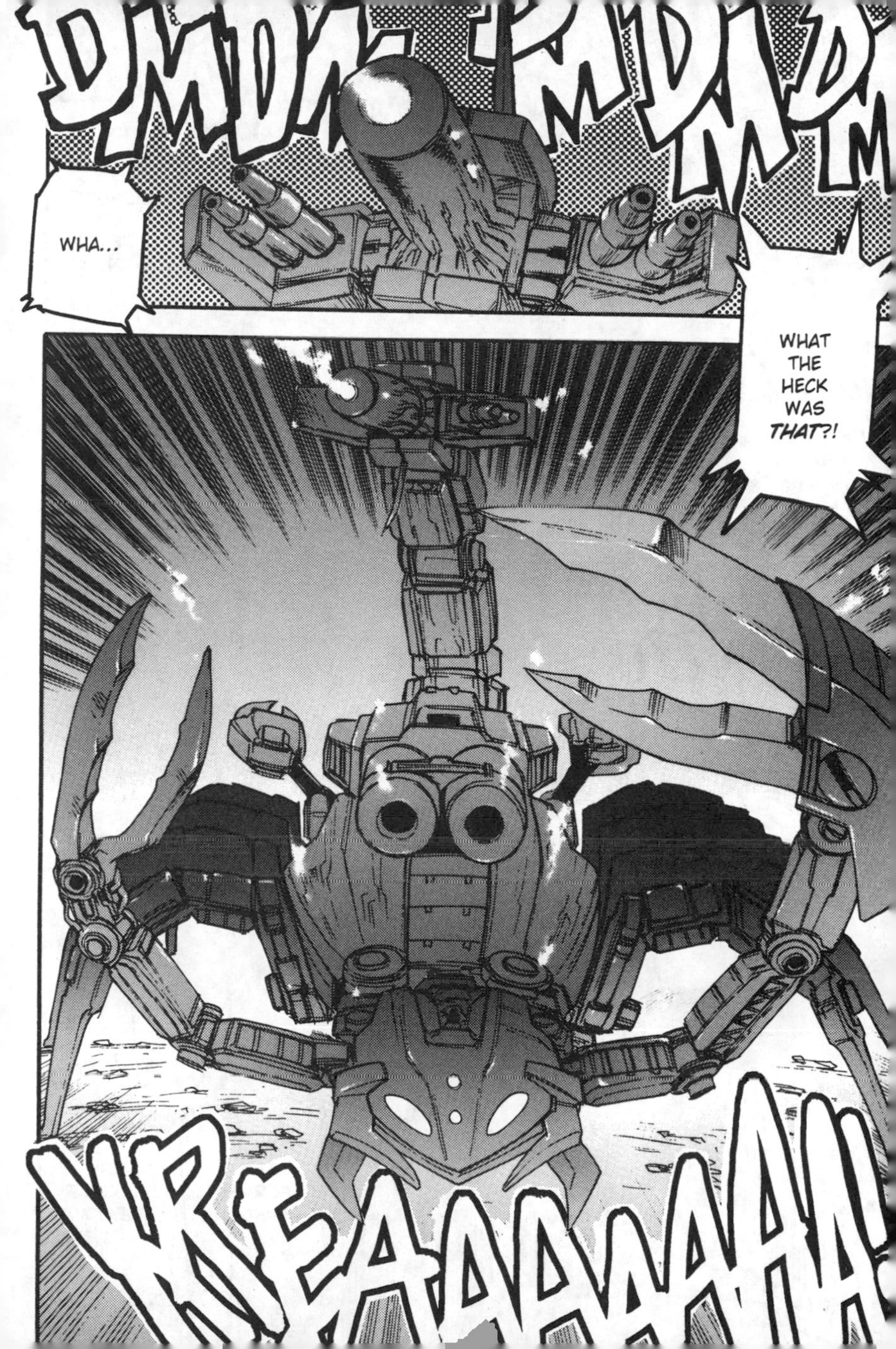
WHA...
WHAT THE HECK WAS *THAT*?!

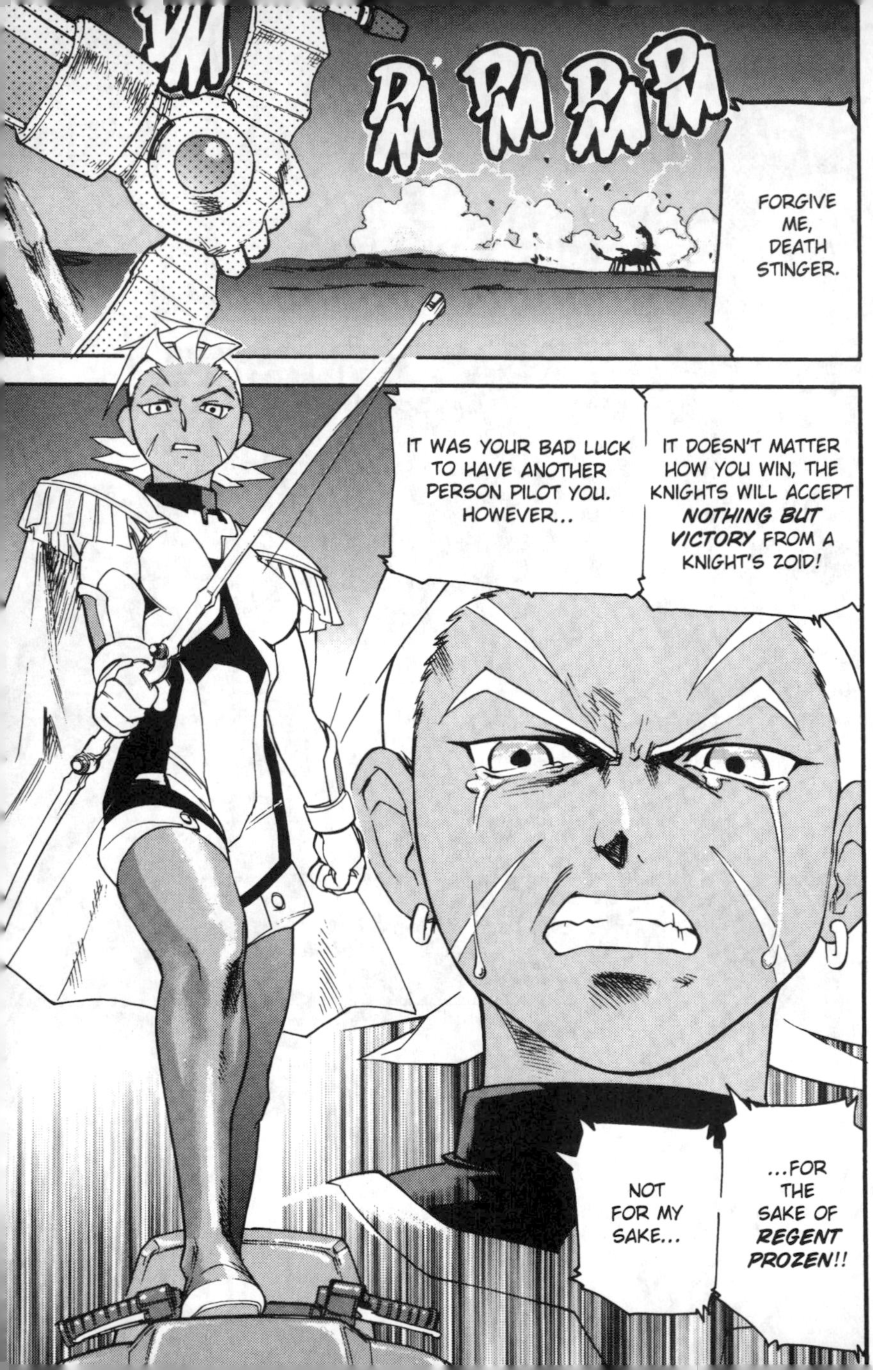
VM
DA DA DA DA DA
FORGIVE ME, DEATH STINGER.
IT WAS YOUR BAD LUCK TO HAVE ANOTHER PERSON PILOT YOU. HOWEVER...
IT DOESN'T MATTER HOW YOU WIN, THE KNIGHTS WILL ACCEPT ***NOTHING BUT VICTORY*** FROM A KNIGHT'S ZOID!
NOT FOR MY SAKE...
...FOR THE SAKE OF ***REGENT PROZEN***!!

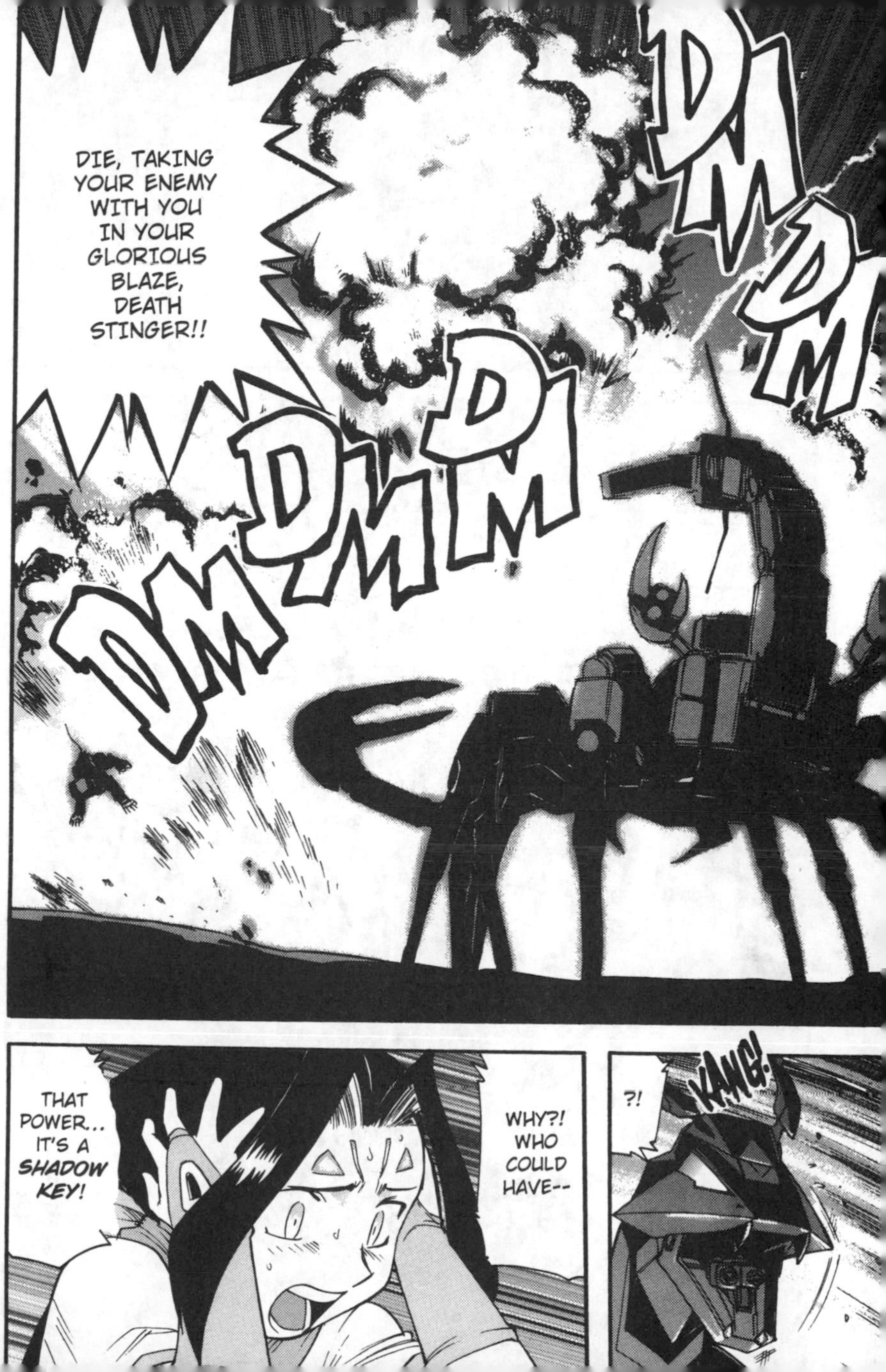
DIE, TAKING YOUR ENEMY WITH YOU IN YOUR GLORIOUS BLAZE, DEATH STINGER!!
DM DM
DM DM DM DM
THAT POWER... IT'S A *SHADOW KEY!*
WHY?! WHO COULD HAVE--
?!
KANG!

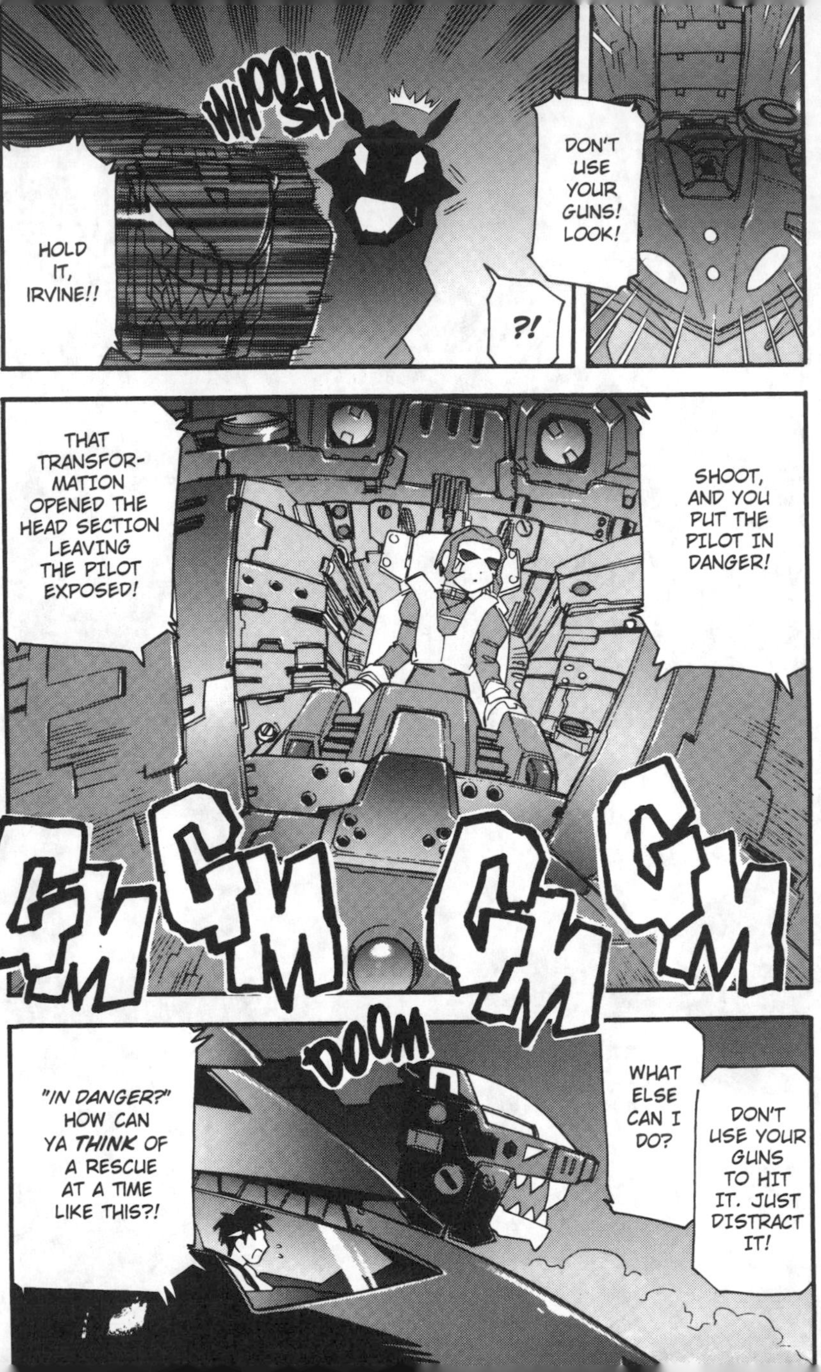
WHOOSH
HOLD IT, IRVINE!!
?!
DON'T USE YOUR GUNS! LOOK!
THAT TRANSFOR-MATION OPENED THE HEAD SECTION LEAVING THE PILOT EXPOSED!
SHOOT, AND YOU PUT THE PILOT IN DANGER!
GCM GCM GCM GCM
DOOM
"IN DANGER?" HOW CAN YA *THINK* OF A RESCUE AT A TIME LIKE THIS?!
WHAT ELSE CAN I DO?
DON'T USE YOUR GUNS TO HIT IT. JUST DISTRACT IT!

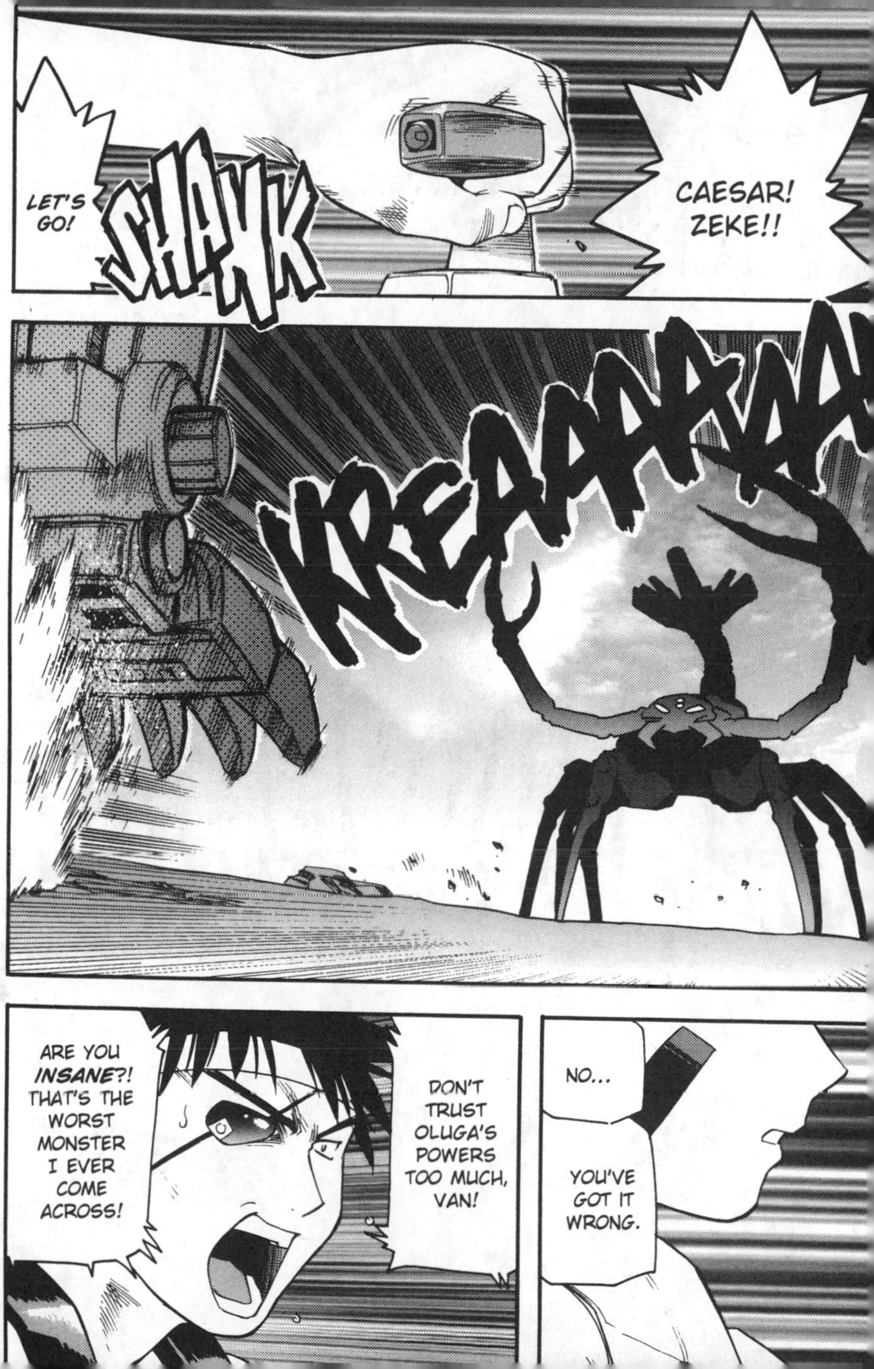
LET'S GO!
SHAKK
CAESAR! ZEKE!!
KREAAAAAA
ARE YOU INSANE?! THAT'S THE WORST MONSTER I EVER COME ACROSS!
DON'T TRUST OLUGA'S POWERS TOO MUCH, VAN!
NO...
YOU'VE GOT IT WRONG.

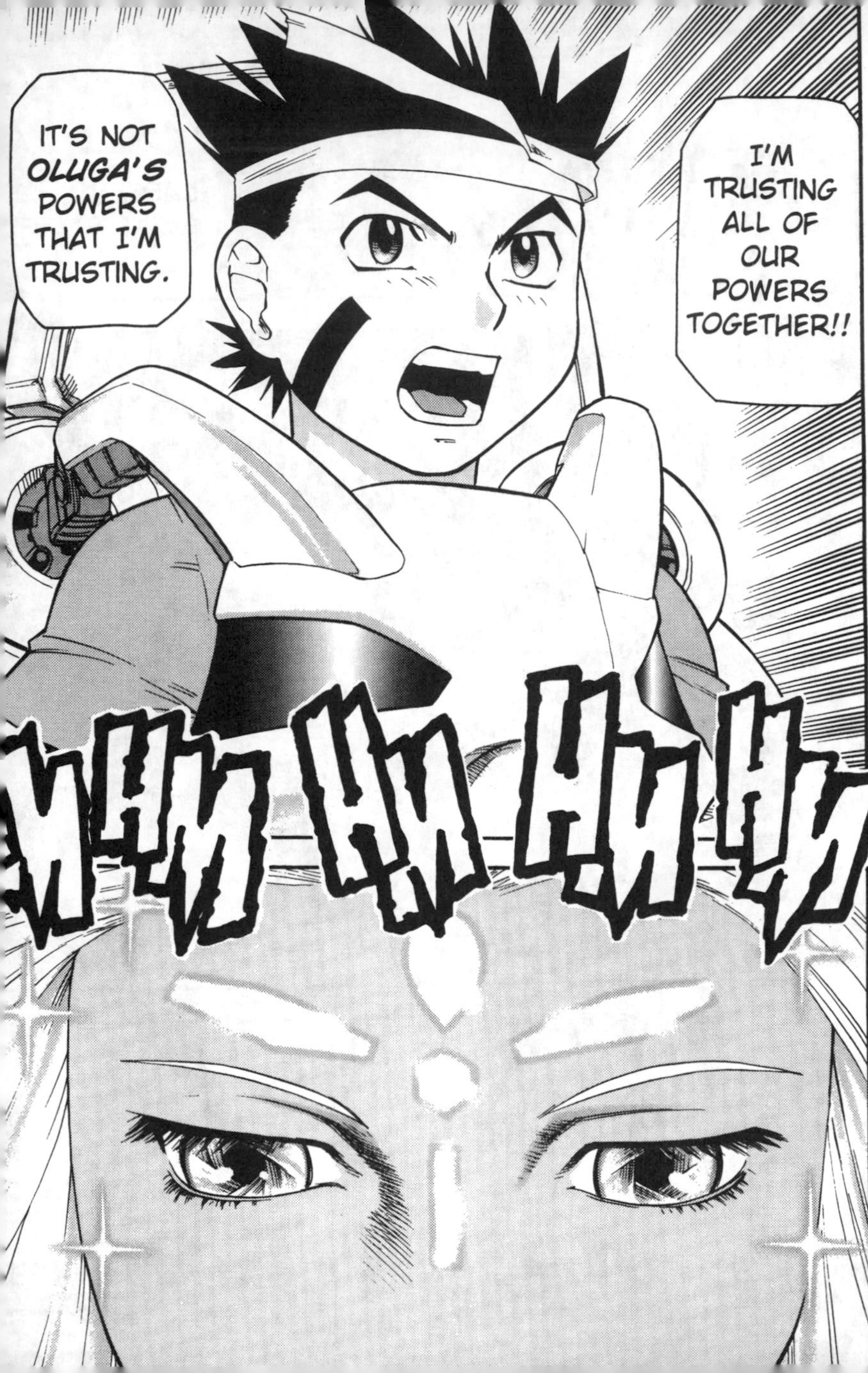
IT'S NOT OLUGA'S POWERS THAT I'M TRUSTING.
I'M TRUSTING ALL OF OUR POWERS TOGETHER!!

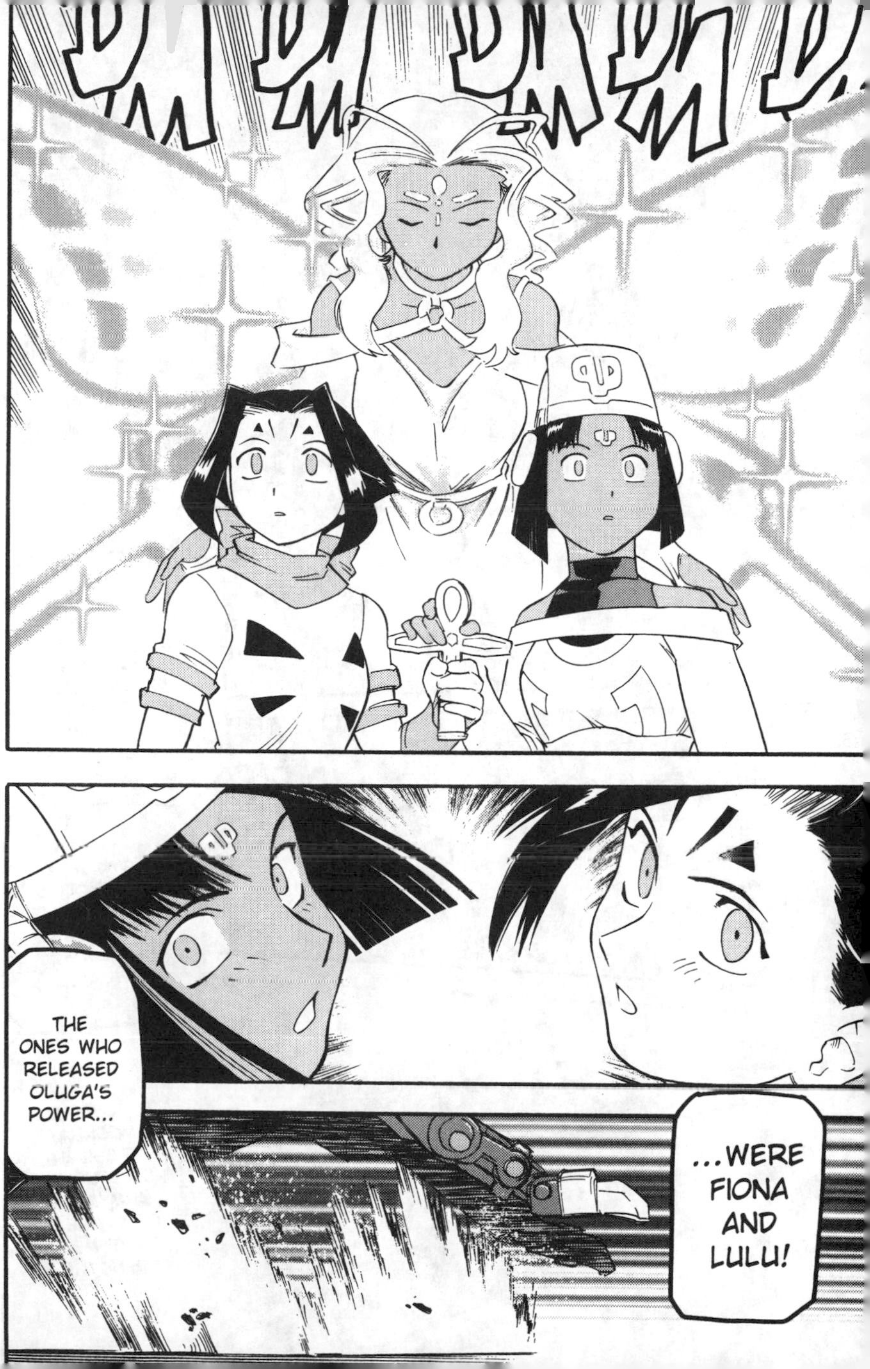
THE ONES WHO RELEASED OLUGA'S POWER...
...WERE FIONA AND LULU!

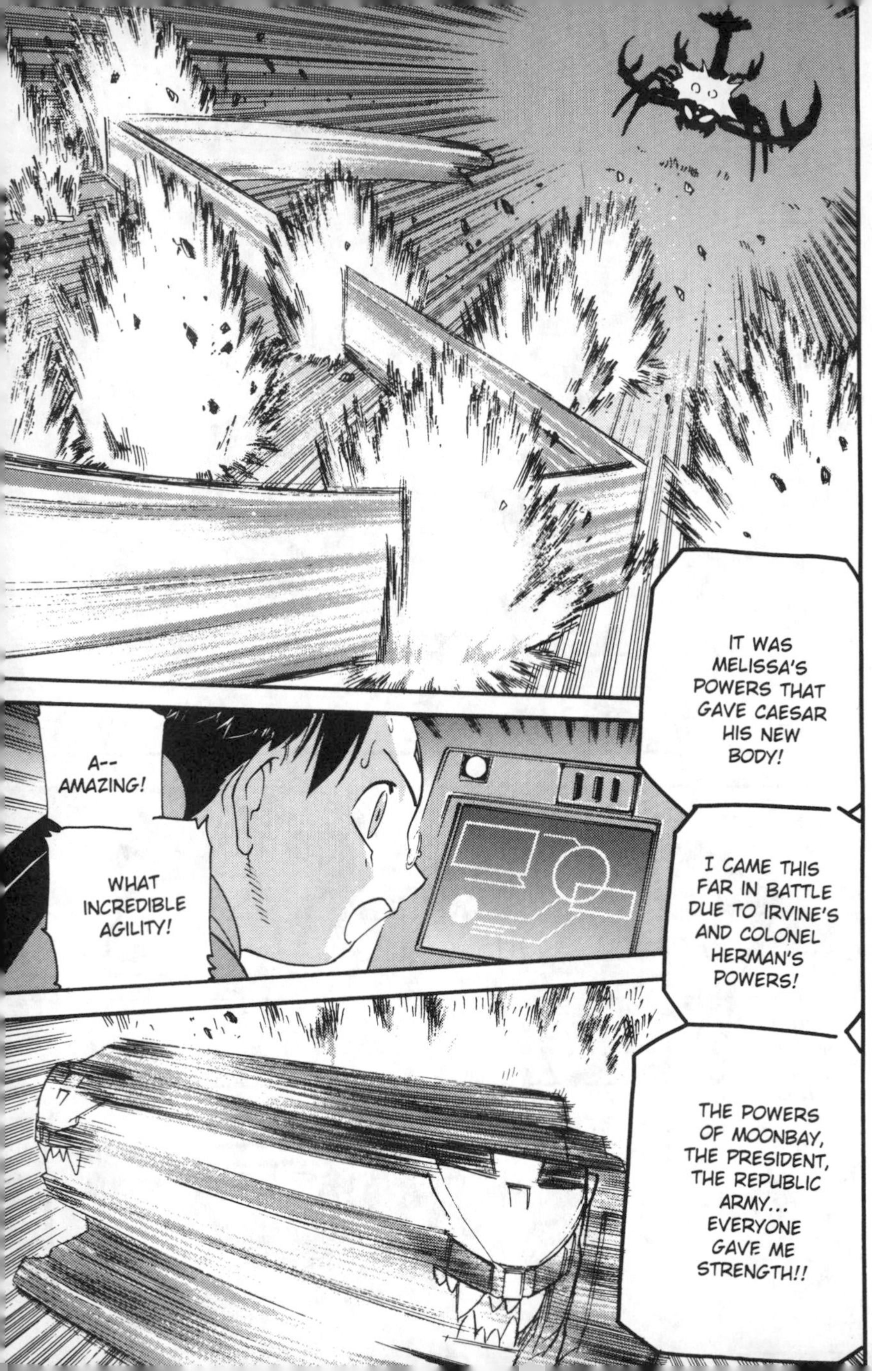
A-- AMAZING!
WHAT INCREDIBLE AGILITY!
IT WAS MELISSA'S POWERS THAT GAVE CAESAR HIS NEW BODY!
I CAME THIS FAR IN BATTLE DUE TO IRVINE'S AND COLONEL HERMAN'S POWERS!
THE POWERS OF MOONBAY, THE PRESIDENT, THE REPUBLIC ARMY... EVERYONE GAVE ME STRENGTH!!

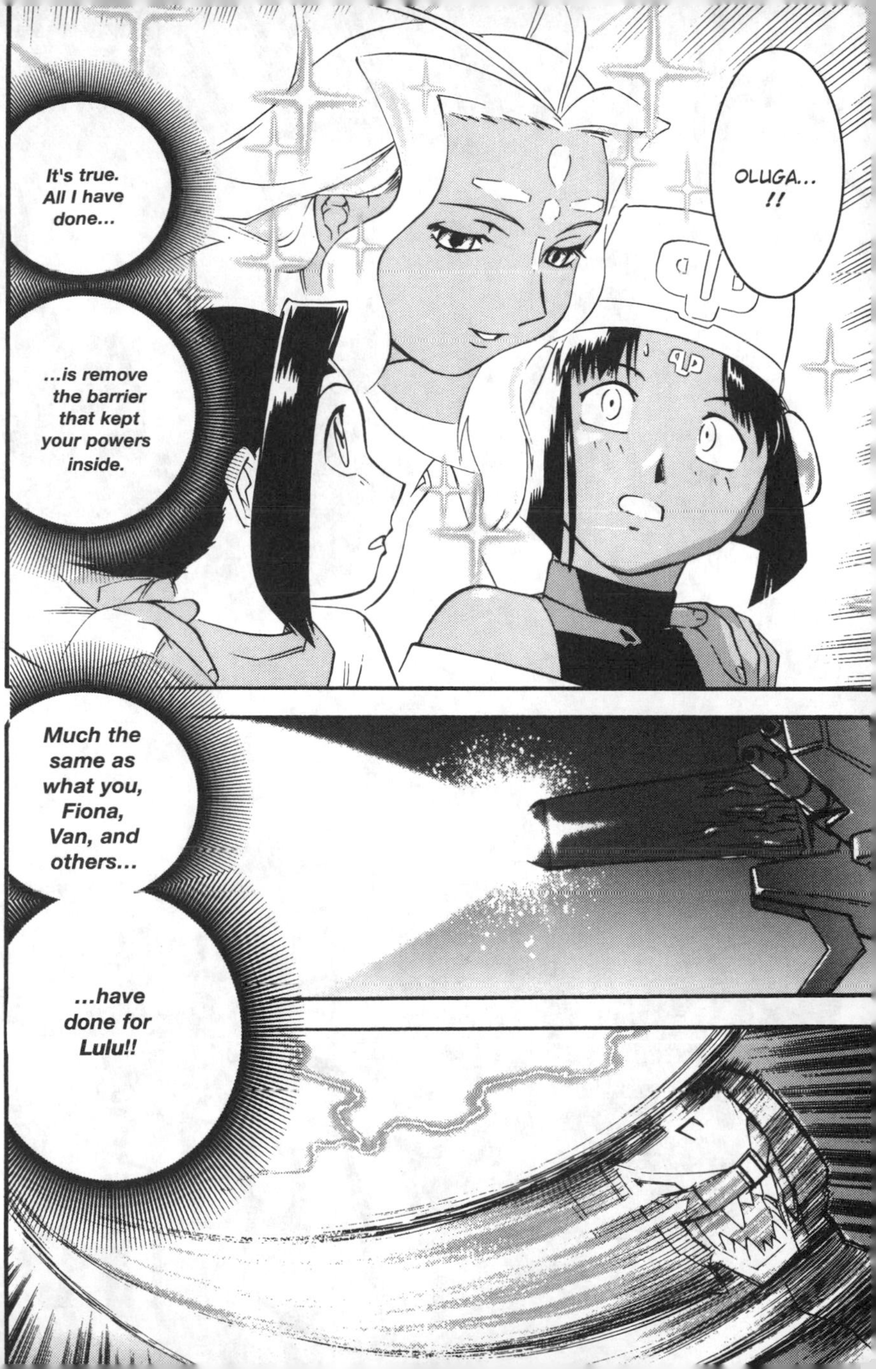
It's true. All I have done...
OLUGA... !!
...is remove the barrier that kept your powers inside.
Much the same as what you, Fiona, Van, and others...
...have done for Lulu!!

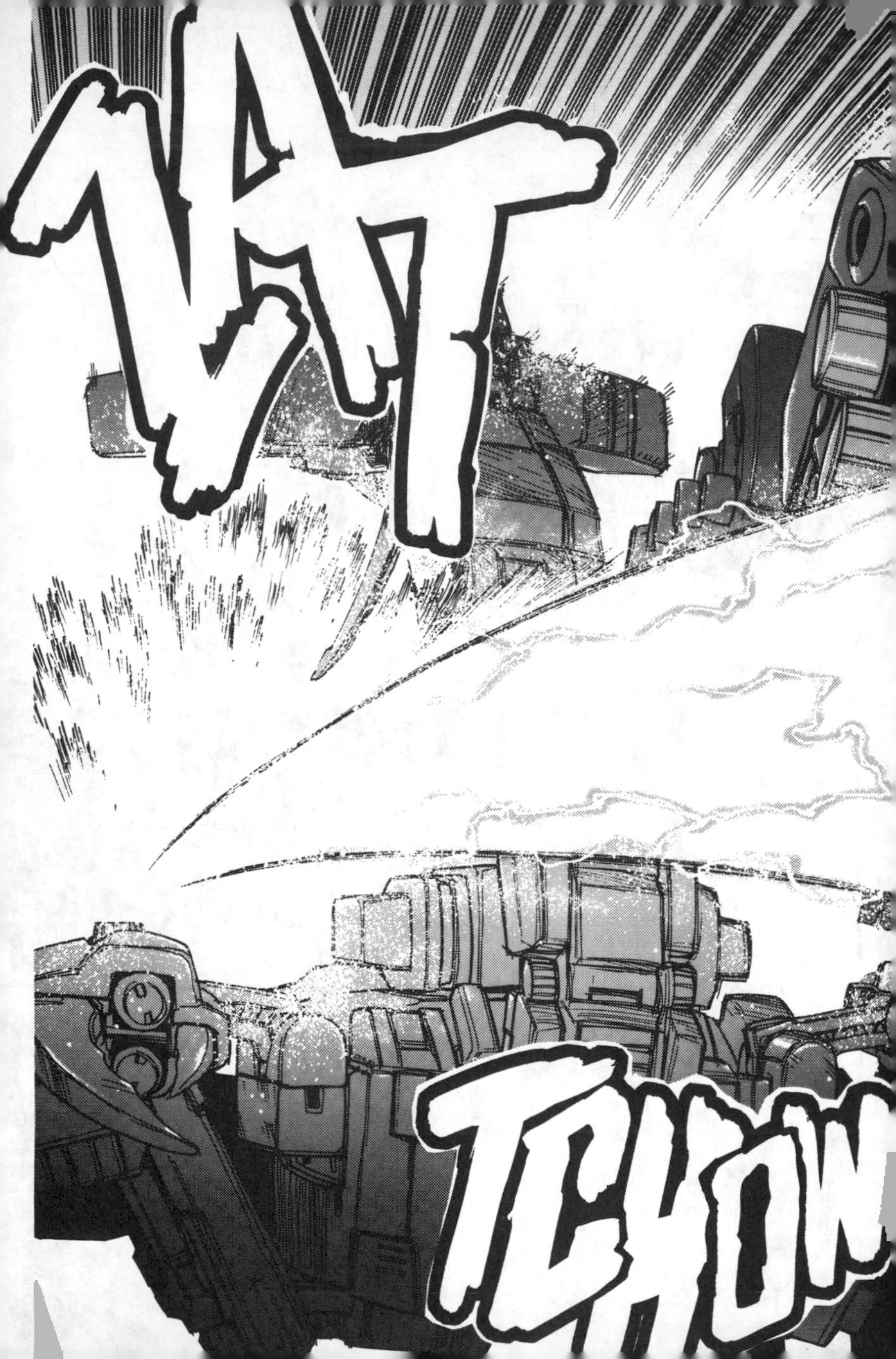
TCHO

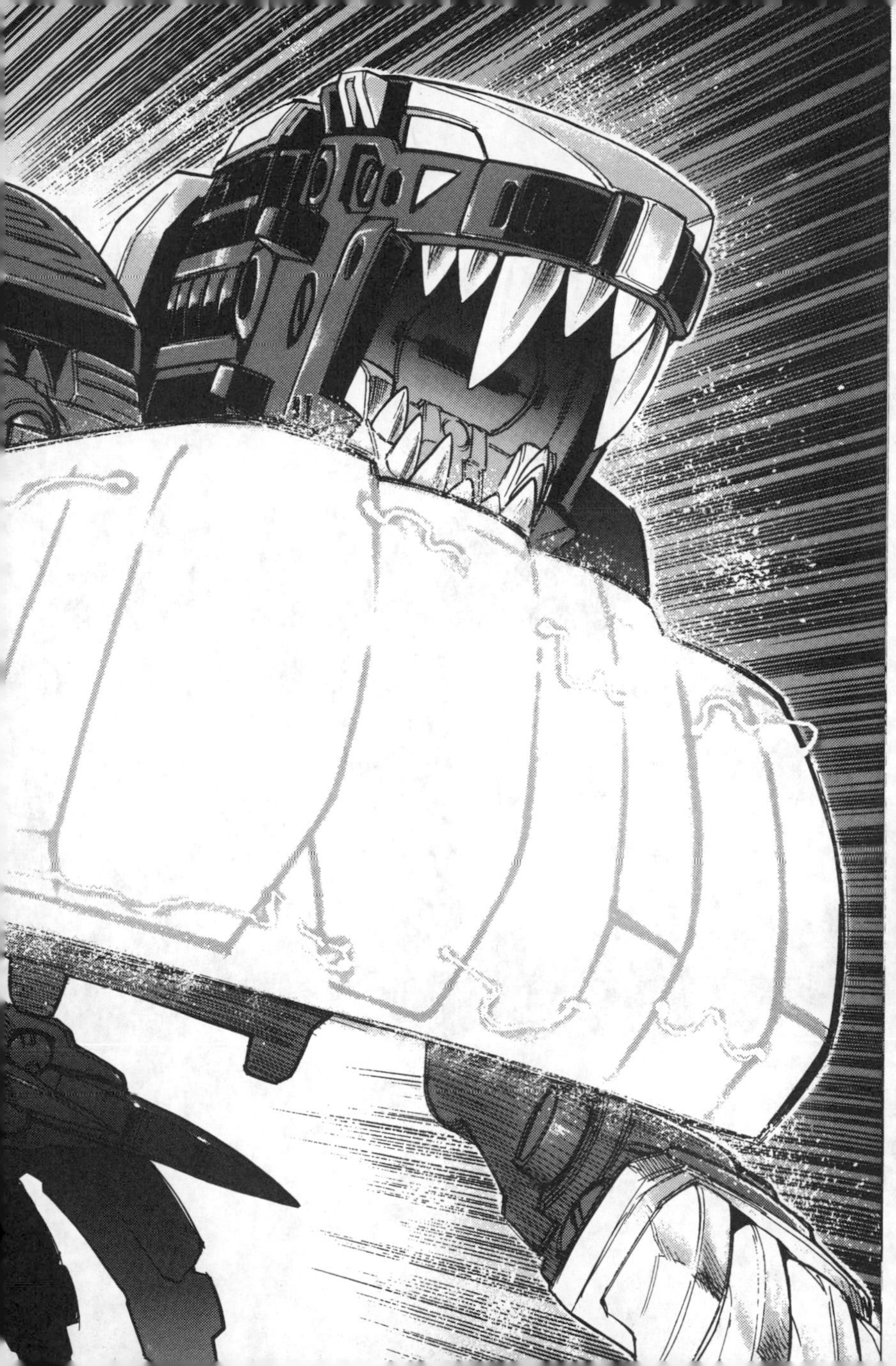

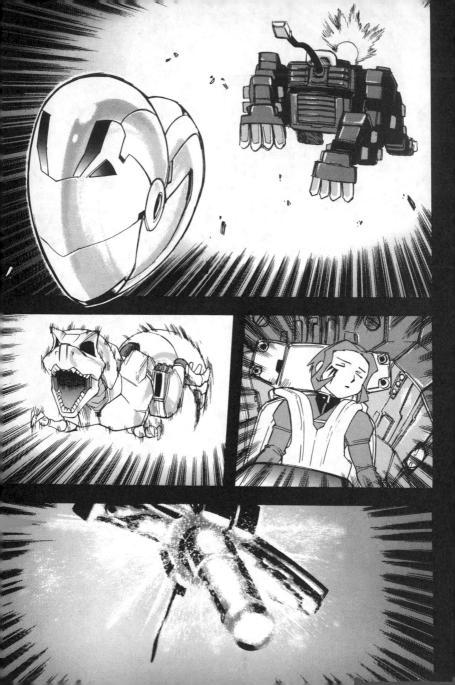

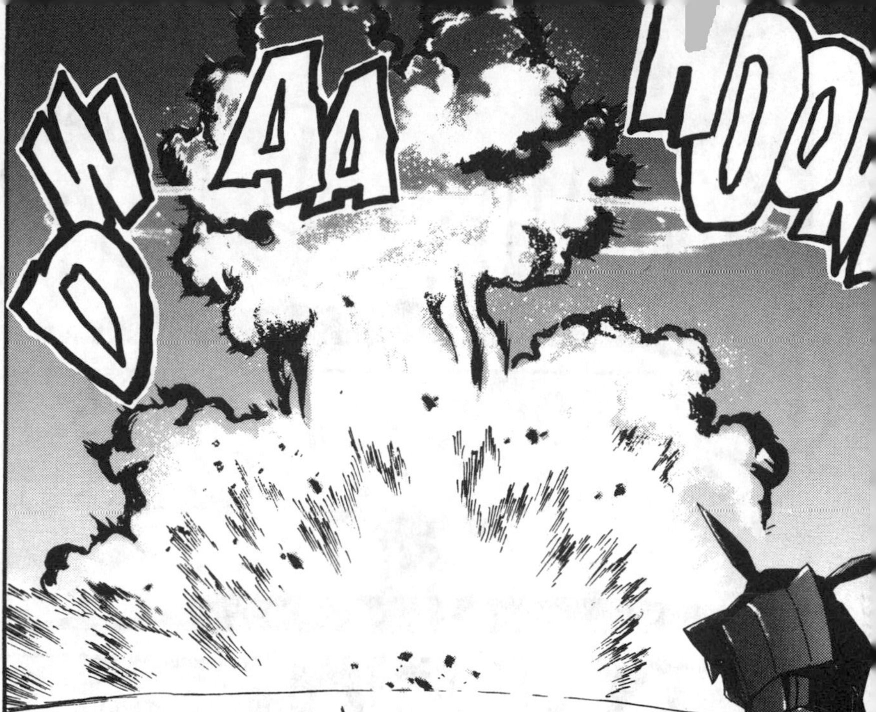
DWAAHOO

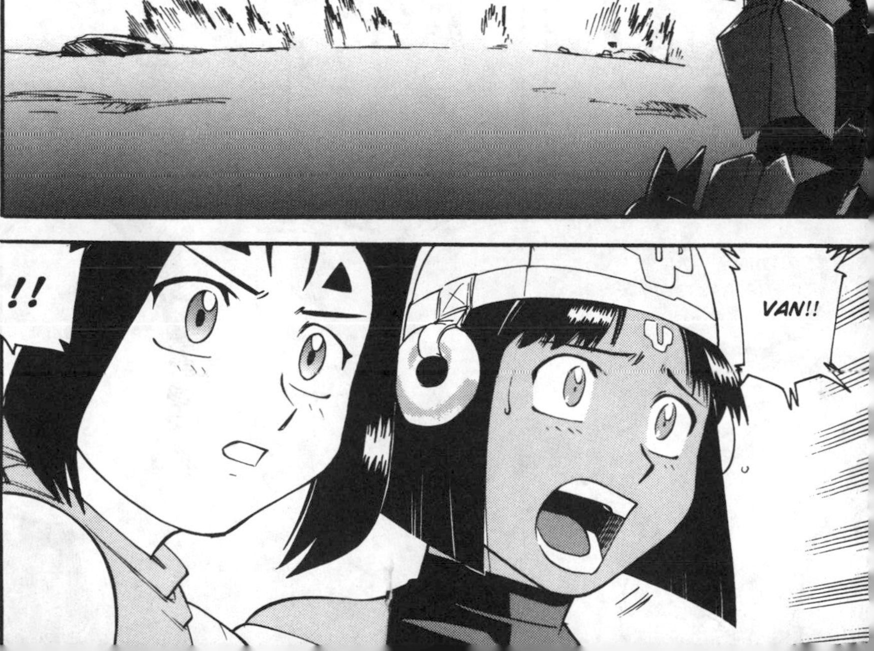
!!
VAN!!

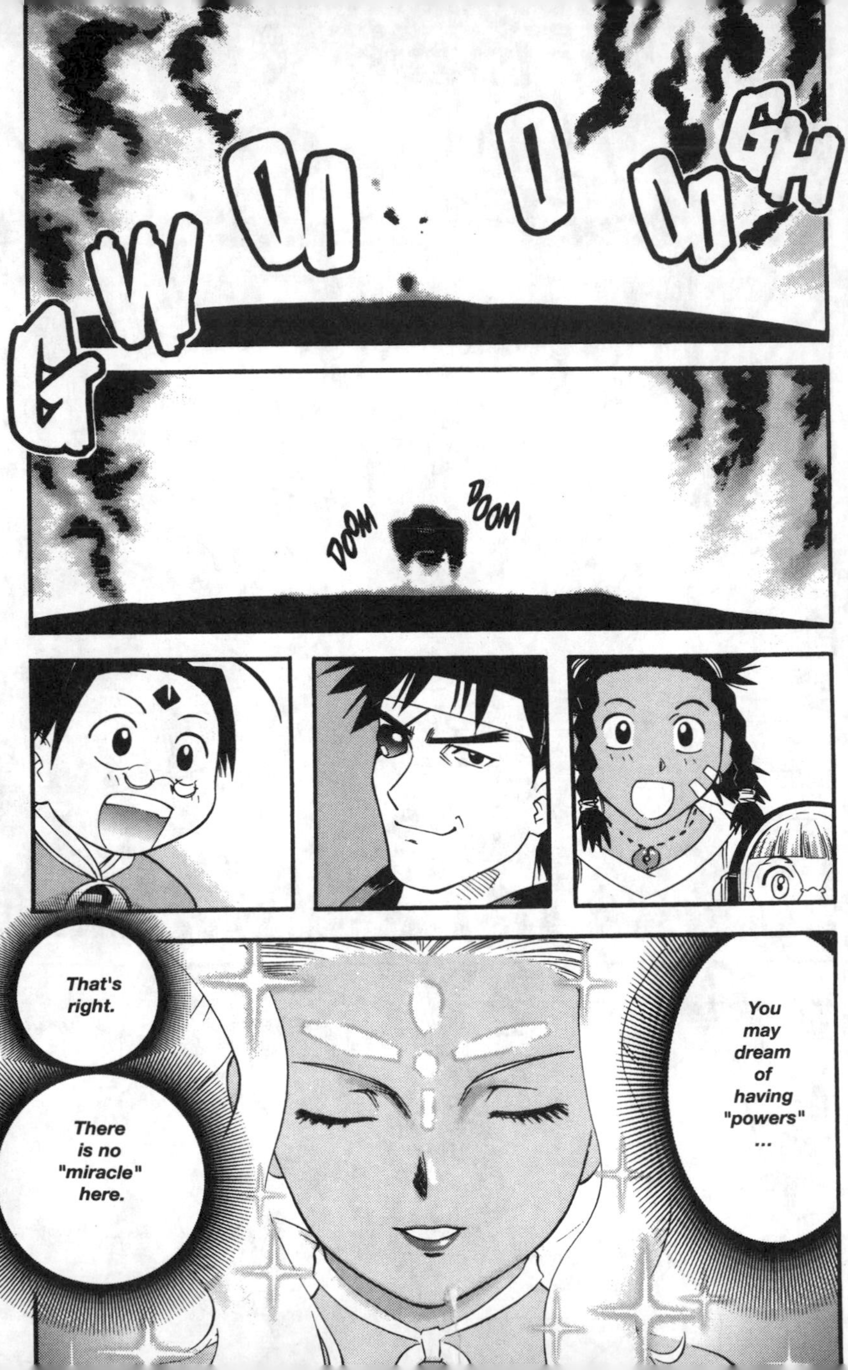
GWOOOOOGH
DOOM DOOM
That's right.
There is no "miracle" here.
You may dream of having "powers" ...

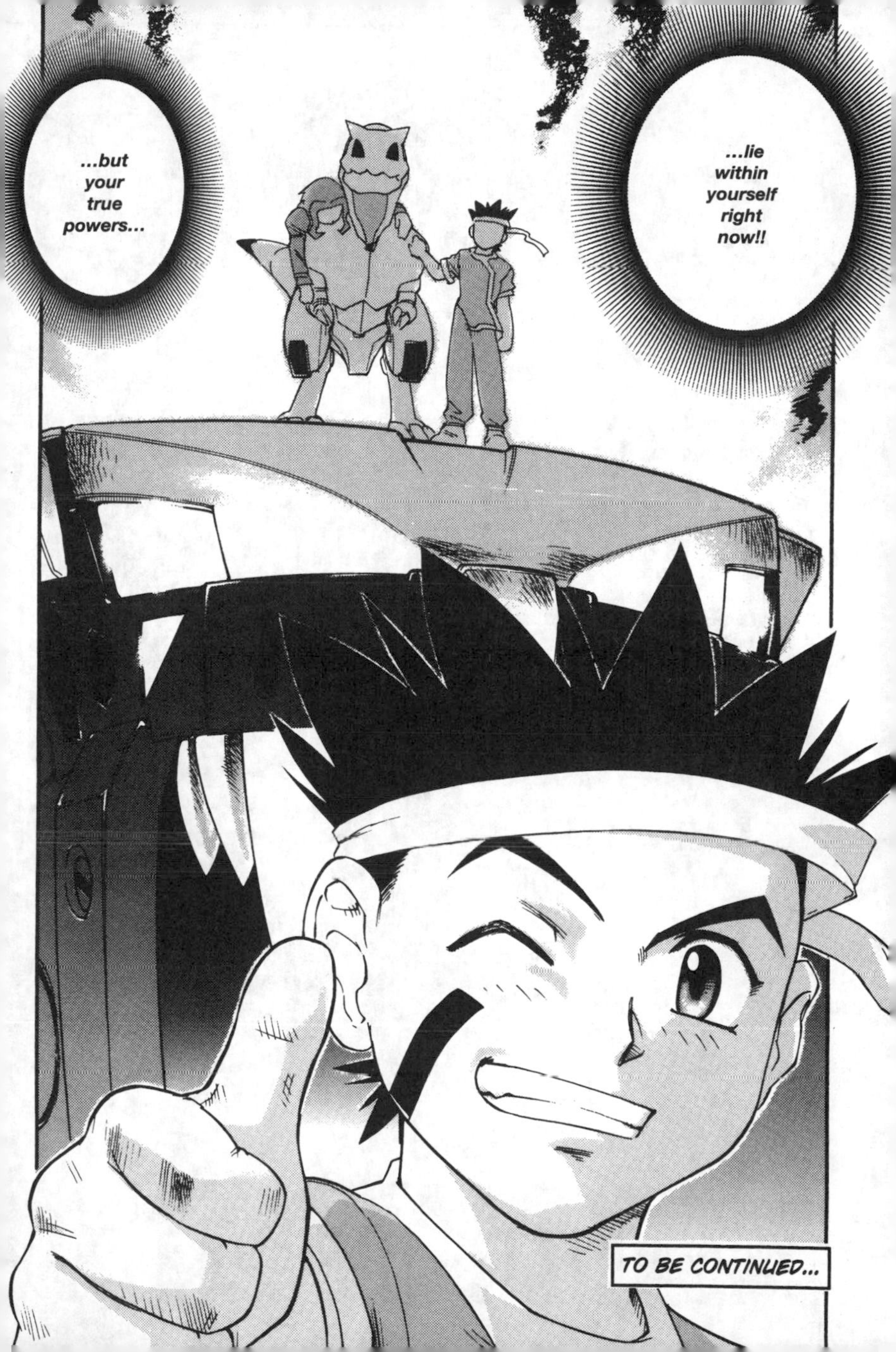
...but your true powers...
...lie within yourself right now!!
TO BE CONTINUED...

The popular robots of the Fox Kids TV series and Hasbro toy can now be found in a comic featuring two new issues every month!

From backyards, to playgrounds, to stadiums: kids and their pet robots called Medabots compete against each other in Robattles hoping ultimately to earn the title of World Robattle Champion! Medabots are robots armed with an A.I. and an impressive collection of weaponry ready to Robattle and win!

In fact, the more a Medabot battles, the more powerful it can become... and the more it stands to lose! Medabots that lose a battle yield some of their Medaparts to the winner, so every battle counts!

Medabots Comic 1 & 2
b&w...40 pages
$2.75 US and $4.50

Beginning from Viz Comics!
MORE MEDABOTS. MORE POWER.

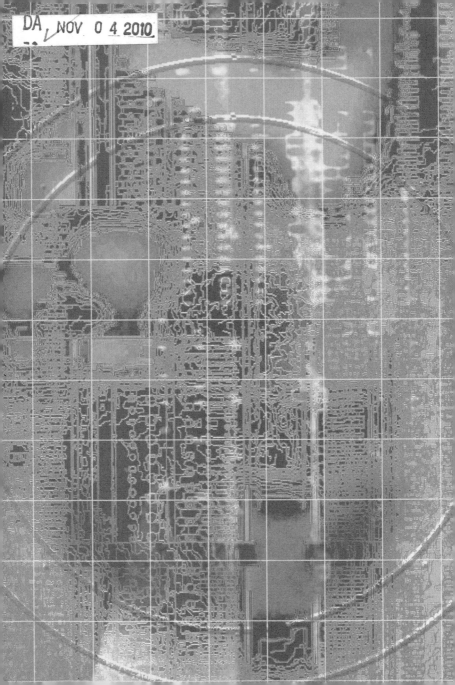